Beethoven's
Tenth

Beethoven's Tenth

BRIAN HARVEY

RAVEN BOOKS
an imprint of
ORCA BOOK PUBLISHERS

Library and Archives Canada Cataloguing in Publication

Harvey, Brian J., 1948–, author
Beethoven's Tenth / Brian Harvey.
(Rapid Reads)

Issued also in print and electronic formats.
ISBN 978-1-4598-0869-0 (pbk.).—ISBN 978-1-4598-0870-6 (pdf).—
ISBN 978-1-4598-0871-3 (epub)

I. Title. II. Series: Rapid reads
PS8615.A77383B44 2015   C813'.6   C2014-906659-7
C2014-906660-0

First published in the United States, 2015
Library of Congress Control Number: 2014952052

Summary: In this murder mystery, piano tuner and unlikely sleuth
Frank Ryan is forced to solve a mystery in order to save his life. (RL 4.5)

*Orca Book Publishers is dedicated to preserving the environment and has
printed this book on Forest Stewardship Council® certified paper.*

Orca Book Publishers gratefully acknowledges the support for
its publishing programs provided by the following agencies:
the Government of Canada through the Canada Book Fund and the
Canada Council for the Arts, and the Province of British Columbia
through the BC Arts Council and the Book Publishing Tax Credit.

Cover design by Jenn Playford
Cover photography by Getty Images

ORCA BOOK PUBLISHERS
PO Box 5626, Stn. B
Victoria, BC Canada
V8R 6S4

ORCA BOOK PUBLISHERS
PO Box 468
Custer, WA USA
98240-0468

www.orcabook.com
Printed and bound in Canada.

18 17 16 15 • 4 3 2 1

Life is a lot like jazz...
it's best when you improvise.

—George Gershwin

Chops

It's amazing what people lose inside grand pianos. House keys, a corned beef sandwich, a single dirty sock—I think I've seen it all, then somebody goes one better. Once I found a black bra between the last three bass strings of a nine-foot concert grand. Not jammed, not stuffed, but carefully threaded, way down at the end of the instrument. Don't ask me why. The owner of the piano was a retired concert pianist about a hundred years old. When I gave the undergarment a tug, a little piece came away in my fingers. It must have been as old as he was. Maybe it was a keepsake. Maybe it was his. You just never know.

So when Miss Pieczynski called to tell me her piano was making a clicking noise, I made room for her in my schedule. I like old people. They don't waste your time trying to impress you. And I especially liked Miss P.

"Is terrible!" she shouted. I held the phone at arm's length. Miss P.'s early experience of telephones had probably been in one of those eastern European countries, don't ask me which. It seemed she had never adapted to phones that actually work.

"Is not Steinway anymore," she yelled. "Is typewriter!"

When Miss P. opened her apartment door, I could hear some innocent Mozart sonata being bludgeoned to death. She grabbed my wrist and pulled me so close I could count the cracks in the powder on her cheek. Her lipstick was off target. It looked like she'd put it on in her sleep.

"Beginner," she hissed. "This one I am teaching only for the money." She tugged me toward what she called her music room while I hopped and stumbled out of my shoes. My toolbox swung and caught me in the knee. "Is okay—he tries hard. And he pays cash." She rubbed a bony thumb and index finger together.

Miss P.'s music room was also her living room. It might have been her dining room too if her piano hadn't been so long. The guy attacking it looked more like a meat-packer than a music student. He was hunched over Miss P.'s beautiful old Steinway, pounding on it like he was tenderizing a slab of beef. The sleeves of his leather jacket were rolled back, revealing wrists so hairy you could have lost a Rolex in there. A knockoff Rolex probably. His fingers were as fat as the Bavarian smokies you can buy on the waterfront in the summer.

"Stefan!" Miss P. rapped the top of his shaven head with a battered ruler. She was old school. "Is enough." He looked up, took me in and cracked his knuckles. The skin around his eyes was bruised-looking, as though he hadn't slept for a week. I began to wonder what Stefan did for a living. She nudged one creaking leather shoulder. "Let the tuner look at my piano. Before you are killing it."

I hate being called a tuner. Tuners tune, and I can do that as well as anyone, but tuning is just the warm-up. I'm a piano technician, and the technician is the person who can make your instrument sing the way it's supposed to. Or make it stop sounding like a typewriter. Whatever it takes.

Miss P.'s student rose. There was a lot of him. An elderly cat wound its way between my ankles and then limped across the carpet into the kitchen. The whole apartment smelled of cat piss and something

4

else I couldn't identify. It wasn't pleasant. Stefan wandered over to the music cabinet and began thumbing through Miss P.'s scores. Every few pages he'd lick one of those sausage fingers. He looked like a guy checking out the skin magazines at the corner store.

"Where's Coco?" I asked. Coco was one of those little rat dogs—don't ask me what breed—but Miss P. loved him. Usually Coco spent most of my session humping my ankle. Miss P. shrugged and righted a faded, signed publicity shot that Stefan had knocked over with his butt-sized shoulder. A lovely woman, smiling, confident, in a fifties perm. The young Miss P.

"Maybe Coco hides," she said. "From Stefan." She giggled. "Now sit. Play. Fix. I have another student very soon. Good student, not like this one." Stefan was still sifting through music scores as if looking for something specific. What would a guy like him be looking for in a bookshelf full of Beethoven and Brahms? Miss P. rapped him on the shoulder again, stuck out a hand and watched him deal four tens into it. She made a fist around the money and jerked her head toward the door. When the door closed she said, "Play something nice. Chopin maybe. You play so good, Frankie. You have the chops."

Nobody calls me Frankie—except Miss Pieczynski. For her I make an exception. The funny thing is, if I'd known what kind of people I was about to start associating with, the name Frankie would have fit just fine. But now I just smiled. *Chops*, for a musician, means great technique, and she was right. As a piano student I'd had chops in abundance. Chops matter. You can have all the talent in the world, but without chops you're never going to have a career. I was the other way around, at least with the classical stuff Miss P. had made her living playing and teaching—lots of chops but not enough talent. That combination only works with great looks, and I flunked in that department too. Then there was my name. Frank Ryan—does that sound like a classical pianist to you? *Frank Ryan Plays Debussy*? It just doesn't work. Franklin might, but that's not what my parents named me.

When I turned to jazz, though, the talent problem disappeared. Feeling and chops are enough. As a jazz pianist, I'm in my element. I'm still not a fashion model, but I have two requirements out of three, and most of the clubs I play are dark enough that I'm just a bent-over blob with fingers. And as a name for a person who tunes pianos by day and plays the jazz bars by night, Frank fits.

"Some Schumann, Frankie? Schubert? Scriabin?"

I don't like being pushed. "Not today."
I sat down. The seat was still warm. It was
unnerving, like sitting on a toilet some
stranger has just left. "Let's go with Sinatra."
I waggled my wrists and tucked into the
opening of "Fly Me to the Moon."

Fly me to the moon, Sinatra sang in my
head. *Let me play among the—*

CLUNK.

"Is the problem I mentioned." Miss P.
was right behind me. I pressed on.

*Let me see what spring is like on Jupiter
and—*

CLONK.

Behind me, Miss P. sighed. I left Sinatra
with his whiskey and his babes and stood up.

"There's something inside your piano,"
I said. "Under the lid. It's doing weird
things to your D string. Stand back." The
lid on a nine-foot Steinway weighs a ton.
You've got to put your shoulder into it
and get the prop stick into its little cup,

because if you drop that lid it'll break your arm. That's one reason I've found so many strange things inside pianos—nobody lifts the lids much.

But I know my way around piano lids. I stiff-armed it up, set the stick and jumped back so fast I nearly knocked Miss P. over. The smell I couldn't identify earlier smacked me in the face. I clapped a hand over my nose. Miss P. pushed past me and peered over her reading glasses.

"Coco," she scolded. "There you are, you naughty boy."

Songs of Springtime

Miss Pieczynski's doggie had been pancaked by fifty pounds of piano lid. He hadn't given up easily. His tiny teeth were still clamped around the D string. I was impressed. Compared to moldy sandwiches and antique underwear, a squashed lapdog went straight to the top of my list of strange things found inside pianos.

"Usually he takes nap on bed." Miss P. didn't seem to notice the smell of death and decay. Maybe she was loopier than I thought. This had been no nap. There was no way even a tiny dog like Coco could worm his way down to the end of a covered grand piano. And Miss P. was small and getting smaller, so she could never have lifted the lid, inserted Coco and slammed the lid on him. Because that's obviously what had happened. I held my breath, reached in and detached the two-dimensional canine. The D string gave a twang as he finally let go.

"In front of fireplace," said Miss P. "He always love it there."

I arranged Coco on the carpet. He looked like a miniature polar-bear rug. His smell was all over me now. By the time I'd gotten back from washing my hands in Miss P.'s chaotic kitchen, she seemed to have forgotten about her late companion. Now she was over by the music cabinet where her unlikely student had been rummaging. But she wasn't just sifting through the yellowed music scores the way Stefan had been doing. She was yanking them out in fistfuls, checking the titles, dropping them at her feet. By the time I got to her, the scores were piled up to her ankles. She looked like someone ready to be burned at the stake.

I righted a framed picture she'd knocked over. A family—a boy and a girl in those funny alpine pants and suspenders, between two grim-looking parents. The children might have been twins. One of them was Miss P.

"Is here," she muttered. "Is still here, must be still here."

The doorbell rang, but Miss P. kept on searching. "Open, Frankie. Is my next student." She tossed another sheaf onto the pile at her feet. I'd almost made it to the door when she let out a shriek. "I found!"

I turned around. She was waving a thick bundle at me. A little cloud of dust rose from fluttering pages. "For you," she said.

The student was going to have to wait. Miss P. was breathing hard, as if she'd just played a Rachmaninov concerto. And she wasn't about to be denied. "Before I change mind," she said, jamming the bundle into my hands. "Today I don't pay you in money." She clutched her heart and rolled her eyes, and I didn't know whether to laugh or cry. She could have been in a silent movie. She certainly had the makeup right.

"Today," Miss Pieczynski intoned, "I pay you in art."

It was quite a performance. I looked at the handwritten title on the cover. *Songs of Springtime*. If there was anything I disliked more than classical music, it was light classical music.

"Miss P., really, you shouldn't." I started to hand it back, but Miss P. outmaneuvered me. She held both arms out, and suddenly she didn't look dotty anymore. She just looked old. And frightened.

I'm not much of a hugger, but if I'd known this was the last time I'd ever see this strange lady, I'd have managed a better one. I gave her a halfhearted squeeze. It was like embracing a bundle of sticks. "Not for money," she whispered into my chest. "For the world."

A check for my services would have been nicer. Piano technicians are independent, and I like that, but they don't make much. But what could I say? When I finally made it to the door, Miss P.'s next student was still standing there. A solemn-looking girl, maybe twelve, in a private-school blazer and kilt. Miss P. wasn't cheap, so she tended to get the students whose families could afford her. The kid looked up at me, caught a whiff of Coco and frowned.

"Take it easy," I said, stepping past her with my tool kit in one hand and *Songs of Springtime* in the other. "She's having a rough day."

* * *

A day later, the after-dinner crowd was just starting to wander into The Loft. I liked playing there. It was just the right size for me, the way Nanaimo was just the right city. Big enough to be interesting, smart enough not to want to be bigger. The Loft had a decent piano that was positioned perfectly. Not so close to the bar that I couldn't hear myself play, not so far in a corner that nobody else could. The owner, Kaz Nakamura, was from Tokyo, where they know how to do jazz clubs. Low lights, comfortable chairs, scarily efficient food and drink. A fishing net covered the back wall behind the piano. The only other ornamentation was a tenor sax, outlined in midnight-blue neon, that hung above the polished bar. Kaz played sax. I liked Kaz, enough that I'd never pointed out to him that lofts aren't generally below street level. Even if I did, he'd probably come up with a convincing reason. Kaz always had a reason. You didn't win many arguments with Kaz.

Since leaving Miss P. and her dog, I'd pounded and wrenched three crappy uprights into tune and done an emergency service on a wonky church piano twenty miles out of town. I was tired. But here I was, down in The Loft. Showered, shaved and dressed in clothes that didn't smell of dead dog, and noodling away. I stuck to mostly up-tempo pieces this early in the evening. The deeper stuff, the what's-it-all-about tunes and the jazzy blues, I saved for later. Third-drink music, I called those ones. I knew all of my pieces by heart, so the only things on the music stand were a glass of beer and an eight-by-eleven cheat sheet of song titles that I sometimes used to remind myself what to play next. Especially after the beer had been replaced a few times.

But I couldn't get Miss P. out of my mind. I could still feel her eyes on my back as I walked out of that apartment. I wound up "I've Got You Under My Skin" and decided to finish the song I'd started before Coco's reappearance. "Fly Me to the Moon" it would be, jaunty and upbeat and silently dedicated to Miss P. Maybe once I'd played it, I could stop thinking about those pleading eyes.

I was halfway through the second verse when a hand entered my peripheral vision, picked up my cheat sheet, turned it over and put it down again. It was a big hand. Sticking out of a pink silk cuff this time, not a leather jacket, but I recognized the fingers.

"Where is it?" A person as big as Stefan, you'd expect a menacing voice. But Stefan's was gentle, almost wheedling. "We know you have it."

I looked up, but I kept playing. This was my territory, not his. I said something foolish.

"What's the matter, you don't like Sinatra?"

The next thing I knew, one of those huge hands was doing something to my right arm, just above the elbow. The other one reached into the piano and grabbed a fistful of strings, like a butcher ripping out a pig's guts. The piano sounded like there were a dozen Cocos squashed inside, and my arm went suddenly numb. At this rate, we were never going to get through "Fly Me to the Moon."

"Where is what?" I managed, but suddenly my arm was dangling and the piano strings were ringing like the soundtrack to a bad horror movie and Stefan was gone. I looked around. The Loft was still only half full, so probably nobody had seen what had just happened. I flapped my fingers and concluded I wasn't going to be playing anything for a while. But I could probably still lift a glass, even if it shook a little. A visit to Kaz's beloved bar was in order.

Piano Wire

Kaz Nakamura was behind the bar. He was actually polishing a glass. Kaz was very neat. He was unusually tall for a Japanese man, with fine hands, a large head and a ridiculous amount of thick black hair, which I tend to hold against him. Despite working two jobs, he seemed to find time to buy exquisite clothes. Tonight he was wearing tapered chinos and an untucked and spotless silk shirt that I'd have spattered with beer and grease in seconds. Next to Kaz, I felt like the guy who'd walked into the wrong party.

"It's clean, already," I said, pulling up a stool. "How about filling it with something that kills pain?" I held up my wounded arm.

Kaz reached under the bar for the bottle he kept for me.

"I never saw that guy in here before," he said, pouring. "Definitely not a regular."

I took a sip of single malt and felt better already. "So you saw his little performance."

Kaz picked up another glass and resumed polishing. "I was impressed."

"Thanks a lot." I took another sip.

"Pins and needles?" Kaz stopped polishing for a moment and pointed at my arm. I nodded. "But going away, right?" I nodded again, and he went back to his glass. "The ulnar nerve is the largest unprotected nerve in the body. You were lucky. He got scared off before he could really hurt you."

"I beg to differ," I said. "It hurts like hell. And all that stuff about nerves—is there anything you don't know, Kaz?"

Kaz shrugged. "It's a common martial-arts move," he said. "I've done a little of that. But like I said, the guy got scared off before he could finish." He looked at me and angled his head slightly at the only other person at the bar. Down at the end, bent over a little collection of empties. Fat and fiftyish, with a gray beard that looked like he'd trimmed it himself. Using hedge clippers.

"The bad guy ran away because of *him*? Come on, Kaz, he's wearing sandals." I leaned out to get a better look. "And black socks."

"I think he's a cop."

"Well, maybe a jazz-loving one." I tossed back the rest of my whiskey with my good hand and lifted the wounded one to the bar, piano-style. I wiggled my fingers, trying out a tune on the warm polished alder. It was a very beautiful bar. A bar that people stared into. It probably sold a lot of drinks. For all I knew, Kaz had made it in his basement using traditional Japanese hand tools.

"Back in business," I said. "Thanks for the drink. And the diagnosis." When I stood, the rumpled guy at the end of the bar never looked up. Part of me just wanted to go home, but another part of me knew that at home and alone was the last combination I needed. The piano was still there, waiting, and another half dozen people had come in while I was talking to Kaz. I resolved to try to forget about Stefan and his fleshy fingers. The show would go on.

Two hours later, I was deeply into my late-night list. The place was nearly full, and everyone was nicely settled in with drinks and grilled soybeans on a stick or whatever Kaz's kitchen had come up with that night. This was the time when Kaz usually showed up at my elbow with his sax. We'd nod at each other, exchange a few suggestions and get down to music.

But the person who arrived at the piano wasn't Kaz. The rumpled guy with the wreck of a beard pulled up a chair and plopped himself down just as I was finishing a song.

"Nice," he said, sticking out a hand that seemed too small for his body. "Bob Brossard. City Police." I hesitated, and he pulled his hand back. "Still sore? Bummer. Could have been worse though." He dropped a business card on the piano lid. "What do you know about a Miss Olga Pieczynski?" He took a long time with her name. No wonder everyone called her Miss P.

"What do I know about her?" I looked over at the bar, but Kaz wasn't there. No help from that quarter. "She's a client. A nice old lady." What was all this about? I saw her again, holding out her arms to me with her squashed dog in the background. "Maybe a little eccentric."

"When was the last time you saw her?"

I mentally counted off all the pianos I'd serviced since then. "Yesterday. Why?"

Officer Brossard was thumbing through a little spiral notebook, the cheap kind you buy in a drugstore and lose before they're half full. He just nodded. "Like I thought. You were the last person to see her alive."

"You're saying she's not alive?"

"You don't read the newspaper?"

"Not if I can help it."

"Watch the news?"

"I don't have a TV."

"So you don't know that Miss…whatnot… was found dead in her apartment?"

It took me a moment. Poor Miss P. Maybe Coco's death really had sent her over the edge. She certainly hadn't looked good.

"What was it? Heart attack? A stroke?"

Officer Brossard looked up. Lots of rumpled guys look kind of friendly, but this one didn't. "Piano wire," he said. "Something I guess you're pretty familiar with." He made two fists, one beside each ear, and stuck out a pink tongue. "Get the picture?"

I grabbed his business card off the music stand. *Sergeant Robert Brossard,* it said. *Nanaimo Police.* There was a little city logo and a phone number. I'd never seen a cop's card before. But Brossard said he was a cop. So did Kaz. I was a piano technician. What did I know?

"I'm with Community Policing," said Brossard, as though reading my thoughts. "Sometimes the soft approach works better."

"Wait. I wasn't the last person. There was a student. A girl. She came just as I was leaving."

Brossard leafed through his little book. "We talked to her. She's in shock. Something about a dead dog." He looked hard at me. "You do the dog too?" He smacked me on the shoulder. "Just kidding."

"You're saying Miss P. was killed."

"Yeah, yeah. Piano wire."

Suddenly I saw Stefan again, going methodically through Miss P.'s music. And those big hands, right where Brossard was sitting now. "What about that big guy, the one who just attacked me?"

Brossard stuffed his notebook back in a sagging pocket. The man was so fat his pants hung way below his gut. I could see two inches of black underwear above his belt. *Tommy Hilfiger*, it said on the elastic. His breath smelled like he did most of his community policing in bars.

"Don't you worry about Stefan," he said.

"I have to pee," I said. And it was true too. Three beers and a shot of fear will do that to you. I stood up.

"Take your time," said Officer Brossard. He crossed his little legs. "I'm not going anywhere."

A Little Night Music

The washroom at The Loft was as stylish as the lounge. A smaller version of the neon saxophone hung above the two urinals, and soft sax music accompanied your own tinkling into the spotless porcelain bowl. Even the air freshener was upscale—I smelled wet cedar, as though I were sitting in a steaming Japanese hot tub. I stood over the pedestal sink, opened the tap and threw handfuls of cold water at my face. In the mirror I saw a beanpole in his forties with a jawline that was beginning to droop and unsexy bags under his eyes. Right now there was water dripping off the end of his nose, and those hound-dog eyes looked worried.

So I did what any sensible person with an unconventional policeman waiting for him outside would do. I toweled off, opened the door a crack to make sure no one was in the hallway and then scuttled out the service door. Kaz would deal with it. He'd probably even expected it. He knew I had no appetite for conflict. I kept my head down, walking fast down the alley past a ponytailed Chinese cook having a smoke against the brick wall and a couple of losers doing a deal behind a Dumpster. I sneaked a look down the dark street behind me. No bald thugs in leather jackets; no portly detectives in sandals.

The first thing I did when I got back to my apartment was open my tool kit and pull out *Songs of Springtime*. Miss Pieczynski's sudden gift had to be what Stefan was referring to when he'd anesthetized my right arm.

Traditional Tunes from Bavaria, it said underneath the title. More like the Bavarian telephone directory, because it wasn't light. But I knew even before I opened it that this untidy bundle with the handwritten title was no phone book. *Songs of Springtime* waited for me on the kitchen table while I made an espresso to help me stay sharp. Then, finally, I sat down and lifted the cover.

It was music, all right. But it wasn't songs. And it sure wasn't for voice and piano, because that requires only three lines: piano right hand, piano left hand and voice, floating above them. What stared at me from my kitchen table had at least a dozen lines, stacked like Greek pastry. Flutes, oboes, clarinets, bassoons. Horns, trumpets, trombones. Beneath the wind instruments ran the strings—violins, violas and the rest, and some stuff along the very bottom that looked like Morse code and had to be the kettledrums' part in all this.

The whole gang was here. This was music for a symphony orchestra. A big one.

That was when I started to get really worried. Not that the music couldn't still be *Songs of Springtime*—maybe someone had arranged the songs for full orchestra. The problem was, this music was handwritten, every note and squiggle, and the ink seemed to have gone brown with age. There were lots of pages, most of them stained and brittle. I lifted the first, and the corner flaked off in my fingers. The neat triangle of parchment bore a faded date: 1825. What Miss P. had given me—bequeathed me, now that she was dead by piano wire—was a very old original manuscript. And some-body else wanted it badly enough to send a Mozart-murdering cretin after it.

I went back to the stove and started another espresso. Sleep wasn't going to happen, not until I knew what I had in front of me. While the pot hissed and sizzled I dug deep into my own collection of music until I found a blank sheaf of ruled music paper. One of the things I'd learned in music school, apart from the fact that I'd never be a classical musician, was how to collapse a symphonic score into a piano version. Kind of a musical shorthand. A dozen pages, I told myself. Transcribe a dozen pages, play it through, and you'll know what you've got. Then you can go to bed.

I poured coffee, grabbed a pencil and went to work.

The first page was headlined *Allegro ma non troppo*, music-speak for fast but not too fast. Standard instructions for the first movement of a nineteenth-century symphony. As it turned out, I didn't need to go much beyond that first page. Transcribing it took me thirty minutes, but by then I knew this was no springtime song. By the end of the second page, I started hearing the music in my head, and by the third I was breathing fast and my heart was making unscheduled leaps into my throat. The fourth page featured some heavy-duty stuff for double basses that would really have been pushing the envelope in 1825. By the time I'd finished that page, my pencil was shaking, and I had to lay it down.

I now had maybe two minutes, real time, of music in piano notation, and there were a few hundred pages to go. I knew how this symphony started, but how did it end? Peeking at the end of a novel is something I normally never do, but tonight was clearly a night for exceptions. I carefully flipped the manuscript on its face, turned over the last page and groaned. There was a big number four at the top, in emphatic roman numerals. Then the word *Presto*. Then the usual dozen lines of densely written notes. But there was no next page.

Most symphonies have four sections— four movements. The last one is often labeled *Presto*. Miss P. had given me only—how many? I did some careful thumbing, and it was just as I suspected. Movements two and three were there, all right, so there had to be one more, another quarter inch of crumbling manuscript. Maybe it was still in her apartment, or maybe someone else had it. Either way, I had three-quarters of something very important.

I stood up, poured myself a whiskey and drank it like water. Then I took the four pages of my piano version over to the piano and began to play what I'd written down. I played softly. Part of me worried about waking up Mrs. Horowitz, my neighbor, who wasn't sympathetic to piano music at any time of the day. But most of me was afraid of waking up someone who must surely be music's most cantankerous ghost.

The Last Breakfast

I woke up to the muffled sound of a game show from Mrs. Horowitz's television next door, so I knew I must have overslept. Although *slept* was hardly the right word, because it had been dawn by the time I'd finally fallen into bed. I had about ten seconds of blissful fuzziness before I remembered why I'd been up all night. Then I rolled off the bed and waved a hand through the socks and dust bunnies under the mattress until it collided with the manuscript of Beethoven's Tenth Symphony.

Because that's what it was. No question.
Even in the crude piano transcription I'd
started the night before, the heroic hand of
Ludwig van Beethoven was everywhere. I not
only had no doubt about who had composed
this music but also knew that a lot of what
had been written about the great composer
would have to be tossed out. Especially those
endless arguments about the effect of his
deafness. Beethoven was definitely deaf as a
post by 1825, when he wrote this doorstop of
a symphony. And if that was what deafness
did for him, I was ready to run out and buy
knitting needles to stick in my ears. In this
symphony, Beethoven had wrung new sounds
by combining instruments in ways never tried
before, giving old instruments new roles and
creating harmonies that would have had his
nineteenth-century audiences howling. After
the first twenty bars of the Tenth, the "Ode
to Joy" began to sound like a nursery tune.

But if I really had my hands on Beethoven's Tenth Symphony, I was still missing the punch line. If there was one more movement, somebody else had it. And that worried me. Because they might have been looking for the first three for a long time. It didn't take a genius to conclude that whoever had sent Stefan after Miss P. was probably the person who had the last movement.

I got to my feet, hammered on the wall for form's sake and dialed Kaz's daytime number. I wasn't sure Kaz ever really slept, because he spent all day running a tiny noodle shop on Commercial Street that did a hectic noon-hour business, and most of the night at The Loft. But it was still technically morning, an hour to go before the first office worker would ding the bell at Really Ramen. And Kaz knew his music. He answered his phone on the first ring.

"I need a second opinion," I said.

"Do I need a new pianist? After what happened last night?" I heard a clang, followed by a gurgling *whoosh*. Pots of soup stock were being upended.

"Not if we play this right. First step, you have to hear something."

"In here?" There was another clang, followed by a shout. I imagined third-degree burns.

"In the washroom. Or your car. Wherever."

I knew Kaz usually worked with a headset on and a smartphone in the back pocket of his jeans. He might easily have been butchering a chicken as we spoke.

"Check your phone in ten minutes," I said. "I'm going to make a sound file for you. A fragment of something really big. Listen to it and call me back."

"This have anything to do with your ulnar-nerve problem?"

"Indirectly," I said and hung up.

I'd left my piano transcription sitting on the piano, all four pages of it. I'd have to learn to be more careful than that. I ran through it a few times, smoothing out the rough spots. My own, not Ludwig's. Then I laid my cell phone on the piano lid, recorded the whole thing and emailed it to Kaz.

It was three hours before he called me back. By then I was hunched over a stained keyboard in a freezing gymnasium on the wrong side of town, trying to bring an ancient school piano back to life. Twenty feet behind me, the girls' volleyball team was having a practice that featured sustained screaming and the thundering of feet. There was no way I could have heard my phone, but at least Stefan or Brossard would never find me there. When I finally got back to my car, I found a text from Kaz. **Come early tonight. Use the back door.**

* * *

The Loft didn't open until eight. "Early" meant around six, when normal people were just sitting down to dinner. I killed some time in one of the coffee shops I haunt, nursing an espresso and scanning a limp newspaper for details of Miss P.'s death. Nothing. Maybe she hadn't been important enough to make it into that edition. Maybe she was already old news. Maybe she wasn't dead at all.

But another name caught my eye. *Man reported missing*, the small headline said. One Stefan Litvak had failed to come home after his job as a dog walker. His elderly mother described him as "a big boy" last seen wearing a leather jacket. What had the cop Brossard meant when he said *Don't you worry about Stefan*? If Stefan Litvak was my Stefan, had the head count just gone up to two? I was reading the story for the third time when the woman next to me reached for her cell phone and I realized it was ringing the "Ode to Joy" from Beethoven's Ninth. What would she think if I told her I had the sequel hidden under my bed?

I got to The Loft just before six, after dithering for an hour about a better place to hide Miss P.'s manuscript. I ended up stuffing it into a manila envelope and strapping it to my stomach with an old belt. It was winter and I was skinny—I could use the extra insulation. And if anyone took a shot at me, he'd get Beethoven too.

Kaz was oiling the bar. I smelled turpentine and cloves.

"Where did you get it?" he said.

If someone called me naïve, I wouldn't argue. But I know I'm not stupid. "I probably shouldn't answer that," I said. "Not yet."

"Take your time." Kaz squirted some more oil on the wood and spread it in circles until the surface gleamed. *The Last Breakfast*," he finally said.

"Huh?"

"You're familiar with *The Last Supper*, aren't you? Well, what if Michelangelo painted another one?"

I thought for a bit. *"Mona Lisa's Little Sister,"* I said.

Kaz laughed. "How about an entire new album by the Beatles? Not bits of junk from old tapes, but a real album? One nobody ever dreamed about?"

"I guess that would be worth a lot of money," I said.

"I guess it would. But nothing compared to what you've got."

"Which is?"

"Come on," said Kaz. He finally put his bottle and rag under the bar and reached for two cold beers. He handed me one and took a long drink from the other. "We both went to music school. In two different countries. What's the common denominator?"

"Probably Beethoven," I said.

"Definitely Beethoven. Did you know the Ninth Symphony is huge in Japan? At New Year's you can't escape it. And you just played me the opening to his Tenth." He lifted his bottle. "Congratulations."

"Or condolences." I drank. "The way people are behaving, this thing might be worth a million dollars."

Kaz laughed. "A million? Just imagine the first performance. We're talking about the Super Bowl of music. And the original manuscript—that's equivalent to, what, the Dead Sea Scrolls? If this doesn't get into a museum fast, the collector market is going to be scary. A million won't even get you to the party."

It was warm in The Loft. The envelope was beginning to stick to me. I didn't want a million dollars, but even half that much would finally get me out of my crummy apartment and into a house of my own.

I thought of Miss P.'s pleading eyes and immediately felt guilty. "I haven't told you everything," I said. "I've only got the first three movements."

Kaz finished his beer. He sat back on his bar stool and looked at me for a long moment. It's almost impossible to tell what Kaz is thinking, but I've gotten pretty good at telling when the thinking is happening. Finally he said, "You think there's a fourth."

I reached down and rearranged the envelope. "Let's just say it looks that way."

Kaz rubbed his small hands together. "I did some googling after I heard your file. Did you know it's Beethoven's birthday in a couple of days?"

"I'm not into trivia."

"December 17, 1770. There's a big international event planned in Vancouver. Concerts, speeches, academic papers. Beethoven 240, they're calling it."

"Lots of people."

"And media."

"So whoever has the last movement of this symphony…"

"Might just be extra anxious to get their hands on the whole thing."

Kaz looked at his watch. "Six thirty," he said. "So tomorrow morning in Tokyo."

All six thirty meant to me was that I had a few hours to kill before my set at The Loft started. With Beethoven's manuscript taped to my middle, I felt like a marked man. But I couldn't hide in the washroom forever.

"I'll make some calls," Kaz said. "I know some people who know some people. Rich people. Collectors. Maybe we can find out who's close to this thing."

"Do that," I said. I pulled my coat around me and stood up. "I'm going to go out and get mugged."

"Before you go"—Kaz held up a hand—"is there anything else written on the cover? I mean, besides the notes?"

I knew the answer to that one. "The cover is obviously recent. Just a phony title, *Songs of Springtime*. That's all. Oh, and something else. A date."

"Which is?"

"I can't remember exactly, but it seemed weird. It was only about a week ago."

What I didn't tell Kaz was that I recognized Miss P.'s writing. She had put the phony *Songs of Springtime* cover on the manuscript just days before she pressed it on me. Was that date meant to tell me how urgent it was?

And there was another, bigger question: why choose me? Did she think bad clothes and an unimpressive job meant that money was nothing to me? That I wouldn't jump at the chance to get rich? Maybe, maybe not. After Kaz had started throwing such big numbers around, I wasn't so sure.

Jazz

I wandered around downtown Nanaimo looking for somewhere to eat and to collect my thoughts. I turned into the Thirsty Camel, ordered falafel and found a table at the back. It was perfect. There was an exit into the alley right behind me, and I could see the front entrance and the busy street outside. I was covered. It was a very Frankie kind of place to sit.

The tiny restaurant was almost full. I shared it with a middle-aged man and his tattooed daughter, a couple of voluble Lebanese teenagers and a red-faced Texan in a black ten-gallon hat who kept trying to show me pictures of his schnauzers. In other words, it had everything I liked about Nanaimo. By the time my falafel came I'd drawn a grid on the back of an ad for hot tubs and was filling in my options. There seemed to be four: ditch it, hide it, announce it, call the police. The last one I scratched out immediately. The police had apparently already called me, and they hadn't made a good impression. Ditching the manuscript wasn't going to happen either, even if I tried to give it a good home by dropping it at a university or a music school, like an unwanted infant laid at the door. The reason was simple, and it surprised me. Why should I just donate this to someone else? Miss P. had chosen me, and she'd paid an awful price. No way was I going to let some pampered academic take the credit.

I seemed to have arrived at some combination of hiding and announcing. I'd already covered the hiding option by donning the manuscript like thermal underwear.

That left figuring out how to announce it, but Kaz had provided a pretty good suggestion. As usual. Today was December 15, and the big conference was on the seventeenth, Beethoven's birthday. All I had to do was hang onto an envelope for two more days. If I could figure out who had the last movement of Beethoven's Tenth, I'd have a better chance of surviving that long.

I finished my dinner and ducked out the back exit. It was already dark, and there weren't many people about. I made the ten-minute walk to The Loft in three minutes flat and was in my chair behind the piano by eight thirty. And there I planned to stay.

Sergeant Brossard showed up around ten. By that time I was into a good groove, my mind staying mostly on whatever tune I was working through. Whenever a snatch of melody or a particular chord progression reminded me of Beethoven, I booted it back into my subconscious where it belonged.

It didn't look like Brossard had changed his clothes since our last meeting. Or slept. I watched him out of the corner of my eye. This time he took a table in a corner, not a seat at the bar. And he let me finish my song before getting up and stumping over to the piano. But he still wasn't going to let me get away.

"Bladder okay?" He leaned over, and I could smell French fries and a hint of wet dog. And whiskey. Kaz served only the best stuff, single malt, so Sergeant Brossard's department must have deep pockets. Now that I thought about it, those were my pockets. I might not make a lot, but I did pay taxes.

"If you have to pee, don't worry—I'll come along with you."

"I don't have to pee," I said.

"Then maybe I can buy you a drink." He patted me on the shoulder, and I moved out of reach. The manuscript didn't stick out far, but even Brossard would eventually detect a bulge under my jacket.

"Follow me," he said.

Kaz came over and took our orders. "Everything okay?"

"Fine," said Brossard.

"All good," I said.

"I'll get right to it," said Brossard when Kaz had left. He took a swallow of whiskey. "We're really at a dead end with this killing. Your friend."

"Client."

"Either way, you were with her the day she died. You must have noticed something." Brossard reached down and scratched himself somewhere I didn't want to see. "Am I making you nervous, Frankie?"

"It's Frank. And you're not making me nervous." But he was. I felt a drop of sweat roll down my ribs. It was getting hot inside Miss P.'s manuscript, and Sergeant Brossard hadn't even asked me anything yet.

"That's good, because you don't have any reason to be nervous. Do you?"

I shook my head.

"So how was she behaving when you saw her?"

"The usual. Miss P. is kind of eccentric. Was."

"Anybody with her? Other students maybe?"

By this time the manuscript stuck to my stomach seemed to weigh a ton. Brossard was picking at his beard and peering closely at me.

"We covered that already. The student who came in when I left."

"Nobody else, Frankie?"

"There was this big guy. The guy who was here last night." I stopped. Stefan had been looking for something in Miss P.'s music cabinet. If that something was the manuscript, did telling this cop make my life harder or easier?

51

Brossard jumped in before I had to decide. "Litvak? Don't you worry about him. He's not a suspect."

"Plus he's disappeared. Conveniently."

Brossard brushed that off too. "Last question. Did she give you anything before you left?"

Brossard's mouth was small and wet. Right now it was slightly open, and he was making a soft panting sound. He watched. I sweated. Suddenly and noiselessly, Kaz appeared at our table. He was good at that. "Time for our set," he said. He laid a drinks bill in front of Brossard. "I need my pianist back," he said. "Officer." Then he grabbed my sleeve and tugged me gently away.

"Officer my ass," I said.

Kaz just smiled. "Let's wait till he's paid me—I need the money. But don't worry. He won't be back."

"You're being inscrutable again."

Kaz steered me to the bar and sat me down next to a young woman working on an Asahi beer. "Tina? Frank." We shook hands. Tina was tall even sitting down. She wore skinned-back hair and a determined look. "Tina is a jazz lover. A real one. She's also a police officer."

"A real one?"

Tina laughed. It was a musical laugh. Beethoven would have loved it. Her determined look vanished.

"Kaz told me about your little problem." She jerked her head in the direction of Sergeant Brossard. The table was empty now.

"He's not a cop, is he?" I said.

"Bob Brossard?" Tina said. "If he's a cop, then I'm Diana Krall." She got up. "There he goes. I'll have a word."

I looked for Kaz. He was already beside the piano, fussing with a reed or whatever it is sax players do. He looked like he belonged there. But then, when he was behind the bar he looked like he belonged there too.

Sometimes I wondered how many Kaz Nakamuras there were.

"'My Funny Valentine,'" I said and slid onto my chair. "And no more enigmatic looks, okay?"

Kaz and I were on that night. It doesn't always happen, dropping into that groove, and it's especially sweet when you're playing with someone else and they're right there grooving with you. But Brossard was gone, Stefan was somehow out of commission, and Beethoven's Tenth was finally cooling off under my shirt. It even looked like we had one of the good guys on our side. When I saw Tina stroll back to the bar and she flashed me her surprising smile and a discreet thumbs-up, I launched into a jivy Oscar Peterson standard, and Kaz swung right in beside me. We rode that tune like hawks on hot air, wingtip to wingtip.

When we finished and Kaz took his formal, shallow bow, I sneaked a look at my watch—12:30 AM. Already tomorrow. Only one day to go before B-day.

Family Photos

The next day I made my first mistake. Maybe I was feeling cocky because I'd survived another day. Maybe it was the way the jazz-loving cop had brushed the bogus sergeant aside. Or maybe it was just because it was Saturday. After spending all week hammering on rusted tuning pins and stabbing needles into piano hammers until my shoulder throbbed, Saturday was always sweet.

I killed the morning doing laundry. I dawdled over lunch and an old *New Yorker* magazine. It was three o'clock before curiosity got the better of me.

I rummaged in the kitchen drawer my cutlery shared with near-dead batteries, expired pizza coupons, and address books so old they even contained names of a girl-friend or two. And keys, not all of them mine. A few of my regular clients left door keys with me in case I needed to let myself in. I found one with *Miss P.* written on its head in faded felt pen. Maybe it even worked. I tucked her manuscript under my shirt, where I'd decided it was going to live until I figured out what to do with it. Then I set off.

When I got to her apartment, the hallway was empty except for a smell—onions with hints of Coco. It was hard to imagine Miss P. dead. Maybe the whole murder story was just that—something Brossard had made up to scare me. Maybe I would surprise Miss P. in her boudoir, applying purple lipstick in the general area of her mouth as though nothing had happened.

The key fit. It turned. But the door wouldn't open. I lowered my shoulder and heaved, and the door yielded with a slithering sound. I wormed myself through the opening and fell into a sea of paper. I struggled back to my feet with yellow police tape around my ankles. Brossard hadn't lied about Miss P. after all.

Most of the paper was music scores, wrenched from their shelves, cracked open, tossed aside. But there were books, too, and what looked like about a hundred years' worth of handwritten correspondence. The biggest music cabinet had been toppled into the piano, and a single mangled piano string protruded from under the lid. I tried not to look at that. Coco was still around somewhere, probably reburied beneath the hills of Chopin preludes, Bach inventions and Brahms intermezzi. The place smelled of decay and death.

And it was all unnecessary. Whoever had upended Miss P.'s apartment had put enormous effort into looking for something I was wearing under my shirt. Maybe Stefan had done all of this. Or maybe it was Brossard who had dragged down bookcases and strewn fistfuls of musical notes like confetti. Whoever had done this wasn't a music lover and wasn't an expert in anything—unless it was violence. He had to be working for someone who had the last movement of Beethoven's Tenth and desperately wanted the first three. And if Kaz was right, that someone probably wanted it before Beethoven's birthday. Tomorrow.

I waded over to a little pile of broken glass and lifted out the framed family portrait I'd noticed the last time I was here. Mom, Dad, little Miss P. and the boy I assumed was her brother. This time I noticed something I'd missed before.

The boy had a birthmark, a port-wine stain, on one cheek. It looked just like a map of Italy. The toe of the "boot" ended at the corner of his mouth.

I righted the picture, shaking out a few shards of glass. Then I noticed another photo at my feet. This one must have been taken a decade or so later. Just the father and son this time, only they weren't wearing lederhosen or business suits. The younger P. was now almost as tall as his father. Both were in uniform. I felt a shiver of disgust.

They were a twisted version of scout and scoutmaster. Younger P. was dressed in the shorts, brown shirt and green tie of the Hitler Youth. Daddy wore a gray belted tunic with black collar, puffy riding pants and shiny knee-high boots. The crown of his peaked cap rose in the front like a lizard's crest, and it bore a stamped iron eagle. He looked like a bus conductor.

But bus conductors don't wear Lugers in leather holsters. I'd seen enough World War II movies to realize that Miss P.'s father had been a senior officer in the Waffen-SS, the armed wing of the Nazi Party. And her brother, by the looks of it, was following in his father's footsteps.

The Nazi photo wasn't the kind of thing you posted on your refrigerator. It had probably lived between the pages of some book on Miss P.'s ransacked shelves. I didn't think she'd mind if I slipped it under my shirt alongside Beethoven's Tenth.

That was when the door opened. I knew I had locked it behind me. Miss P.'s place was a typical third-floor apartment—only one way in or out. Unless you counted the balcony, but three floors were three floors, and I'm a piano technician, not Bruce Willis. I turned and watched Bob Brossard close the door behind him and tromp toward me through the spilled papers. He had a fat man's heavy breathing—maybe he'd run up all three flights of stairs. Whatever Tina had said to him the night before, he seemed to be ignoring it. He didn't look amused.

"Not going to try and be a hero, are you?" Up close Brossard smelled like fast food and mildew. He didn't look violent, just unpleasant. My fastidious side wanted no part of a wrestling match with him, and the farther away he was, the less chance there was that he would discover the manuscript under my shirt. I scolded myself for backing down from a small wheezing man in sandals. Then I backed down.

"You're not a cop."

"Technically true." Brossard collapsed on Miss P.'s piano stool. The stool groaned. "I am no longer an officer. But I remember the first rule of interrogation: ask nicely." He twisted his stubbled face into an insincere smile. "Where is it?"

I resisted the temptation to say *Where is what?* But I couldn't come up with any alternatives. So I said nothing. Brossard abandoned the smile and tried another tack.

"Why are you here at all?"

Another good question, and harder to answer. Even if I'd wanted to tell him the truth, I wasn't sure what it was. There was no good reason for me to be in a dead woman's apartment. I'd gotten up on a Saturday morning, let my curiosity get the better of me and here I was. Thinking things through has never been one of my strong points. I had the sinking feeling it was a bit late to start working on it now.

"Two options then." Brossard seemed to be talking to himself. "One, he doesn't have it. Two, he does, so he's looking for something else." He stood up slowly, bracing his hands on his knees. "Both alternatives interest me. But we can't explore them here." He pulled a handgun halfway out of his coat pocket, holding it between thumb and forefinger. I saw a black rubberized grip and a trigger guard. My bowels went watery.

"Turn left when you leave the apartment. No elevator. Take the emergency stairs down to the parking level, left again, stall 131. Look for a brown Jeep, needs a wash." He kicked me in the ankle with a sandaled toe. "I'm right behind you. And I haven't forgotten how to shoot."

Cottage Country

The Jeep was filthy, as though Brossard had spent the last month on logging roads. But I could still make out the cheap decal that ran across the back window. *Experdited Solutions Inc*. There was a Nanaimo phone number. I was being abducted by an ex-cop who couldn't spell.

"Get in." Brossard was right behind me. For a wide man, he moved quietly. He yanked a rear door open just as a man stepped out from behind a van in the next aisle. Big. Bald. Stefan. He started walking rapidly toward us.

"I said get in." Brossard had his other hand on the revolver now. Running wasn't an option, even if I could have got my legs to work. I fell awkwardly onto a mess of Dairy Queen wrappers, and Brossard slammed the door after me. The Jeep stank of vinegar and grease, and its front seats were fenced off by a metal grid. I didn't know whether Brossard was in the habit of giving rides to big dogs or dangerous humans. Either way, I was in a cage. I gave the door handle a halfhearted yank, but I already knew it wouldn't open. Kiddie locks. I was trapped.

Not that I wanted to be outside the car either, the way Stefan and Brossard began to go at it. It was like a nature documentary, the kind I stared at when I couldn't get to sleep on my nights off. First they went nose to nose. Then they did some roaring, most of which overlapped so I couldn't make out any words. Both of them kept jabbing a finger in my direction. Then they separated. Brossard pulled his gun.

I didn't want to see what happened next. Maybe Brossard would shoot Stefan, or maybe they would just yell each other to death. I slid down beneath the window, and my face ground into a wet Tim Hortons cup.

And then...nothing. I counted to ten and peeked over the doorframe. Brossard and Stefan were walking rapidly in the direction of Stefan's van, arms waving and heads together. They disappeared behind the van. One one thousand, two one thousand—and Brossard reappeared, stuffing the gun into a flapping pocket and covering the distance faster than any fat man had the right to move. He threw himself behind the wheel, and the Jeep shot toward the exit. I risked a look back. Stefan was on his hands and knees.

Brossard was making more nature-documentary sounds. This time he was several whales surfacing. "I thought he was competition." Puff. "Turns out he was

insurance." Blow. "The bastards sent backup."
Long wheeze. "Well, I just put him on the
injured reserve list." We hit Front Street and
made in the direction of the highway. I scrab-
bled for a seat belt, but it looked like dogs
and criminals didn't get them.

"Good of you not to kill him."

"These guys have deep pockets. They'd
just send someone else."

Brossard gunned the Jeep past knots
of Christmas shoppers hurrying through
the failing light, ran a red and veered
suddenly to take the long service road that
followed Newcastle Channel all the way to
the Nanaimo–Vancouver ferry terminal.
Vancouver was where I would be tomorrow
if I managed to get out of this mess.
Brossard wrenched us down a side street,
and I rolled around in my kennel. The street
ended abruptly at the water, and Brossard
ran the truck into a vacant spot in a parking
lot that was mostly taken up with fishing

boats in wooden cradles. Nanaimo had a lot of shipyards—this must be one of them. I wasn't a boat person.

"Down the ramp, last boat on the right." Brossard prodded me along a decrepit dock until we reached a battered aluminum fourteen-footer that looked as though it had been dragged here over dry land. Without a trailer. He gave me an extra shove.

"Sit. Stay." At least he didn't tell me to roll over. "And clean the otter shit off the seat." He threw me a sopping rag and bent to untie the boat.

Now was my chance. For an instant Brossard's broad back was turned, but making decisions in instants is another of my not-so-strong suits. I got another opportunity when he began to yank savagely on the outboard motor's starter cord. Again my response was…nothing.

In that moment I knew that if I was going to get away from this guy, Ludwig's precious manuscript still taped to my middle, it would have to be by using my head, not my body. And I was surely as smart as he was. Maybe even smarter, but not by much. If I was really smart, I'd still have been in the Laundromat pretending to read a book while I looked at pretty girls, not cowering in a leaky boat in the dark. But if Brossard had had the sense to search me, he'd have been out of my life an hour ago. We were both a little pathetic.

When the engine caught, Brossard slapped it into forward gear and spun the little boat on its ear. We straightened, flashed through a narrow corridor of looming metal boathouses and then banked hard right onto the ruffled blackness of Newcastle Channel. The front section of the boat was cluttered with sodden life jackets, fuel cans and a crumpled tarp, so I had to face my captor at the back of the boat. Our knees knocked together as the little boat rattled up the channel and I watched our wake unfold in a never-ending V.

So far I knew where we were, although it was the first time I'd ever been on the water. The long string of Nanaimo's marinas spooled past on our right. The dark mass on the left had to be Newcastle Island, all of it parkland, all of it uninhab-ited. Not to mention riddled with the shafts of the abandoned coal mines I'd read about when I first moved to Nanaimo. I hoped tonight wasn't going to be my first visit.

But we didn't bend left at Newcastle. Brossard kept us heading south, and now I had the whole Nanaimo skyline to marvel at. I had to admit the little city looked magical at dusk. The condo towers on the waterfront, so awkward in daytime, had become wedding cakes of red and green Christmas lights, and the dark water of the harbor shimmered. We must have been more or less right across from Kaz's little bar right then.

"No jazz tonight," shouted Brossard, as though reading my thoughts. "Tonight you've got an audience of one." The boat swerved suddenly. Brossard cursed and clawed at the control handle, and I was thrown hard against a stinking crab pot. Then we straightened, and he opened the throttle again.

"What was that?"

"Log. They escape off the boom all the time. Hit one of those and it's goodbye propeller."

"Log boom?"

"In front of your goddamn nose!" I followed his stabbing finger and made out the boom, an unlit carpet of raw timber spread at the doorstep of another island that seemed mysteriously to have arisen on our left just as Newcastle disappeared. Unlike Newcastle, lights dotted the shoreline here and there, but there were long gaps, like a smile with missing teeth. The brightest spot was a red neon sign that said simply *PUB*. So this was Protection Island. Protection had a pub, but in ten years I'd never taken the ferry across the harbor to check it out. Maybe that was about to change.

We droned past private docks and porch lights, the log boom so close I could smell the floating trees. There was still plenty of forest on the island, and the trees were eerily backlit by the lights and smoke of the paper mill south of the city. Suddenly Nanaimo seemed uncomfortably far away.

"Don't tell me. You've never been to Protection Island." Brossard was laughing. He dodged another rogue log and cut closer to the rocks lining the shore. If the log was invisible, so were we. The little boat had no running lights. He bent the boat into a long left turn around a lighthouse, and the lights of Nanaimo swept around behind us. The V of our wake glittered.

"I thought it was just wackos and hippies," I shouted back. "And a pub."

"Oh, we have a wacko or two. And a half-dozen PhDs too. But the nice thing about Protection Island? People let you be yourself."

Brossard just being himself was something I could do without. Now the long turn was over, Nanaimo had disappeared and he was finally slowing, heading for a stretch of uninhabited shoreline. I caught the distant twinkle of a ski hill in the mountains above Vancouver, thirty miles away. We'd done a one-eighty around the end of Protection Island. Now there was nothing out there except the open water of the Strait of Georgia. I didn't feel very protected.

Brossard cut the engine, and the boat ground softly into a pebble beach. He poked me with a paddle, and I stumbled into ankle-deep freezing water. "Pay attention. We've got a little walk ahead of us. I know the paths; you don't. There's nobody around this time of year anyway—they've all gone to Mexico. You and I are going to have a chat. Then I'll drop you at the pub, and you can catch the last ferry back to Nanaimo. You might even have time for a beer."

"And if I don't cooperate?" I felt silly even saying it.

"I'll drop you down a mine shaft."

For a moment I thought about making a break for it right there. Take a dive into the bush and hope for the best in the few seconds before Brossard's experience and the gun in his pocket caught up with me. Or just take a sudden swing. I was a foot taller, and if I caught him right under the chin—but that was ridiculous. And I knew it. I'd never taken a swing at anyone in my life, sudden or otherwise, and I wasn't about to start now.

But I still had my wits. When things went wrong, I usually reasoned my way out, just the way I figured out which three screws to adjust when somebody's F above middle C started to rattle. I still had the manuscript, and it was obviously worth hanging on to. I was a lousy fighter, so I'd have to reason my way out of whatever surprise Brossard had in store for me. I was down but not out.

That was before he showed me his septic tank.

The Iron Maiden

Brossard prodded me along a narrow path. I tripped over roots and rocks, picked myself up, snagged my jacket on last year's blackberry canes and blundered into overhanging branches. So far my instincts had been sound. Making a run for it there would have been laughable. Behind me, a fistful of keys clipped to Brossard's belt jingled with every step he took.

Then we stood in a crude clearing in the forest, the trees thinned just enough to accommodate a leaning, carport-sized building I figured was Brossard's cottage.

I could just see a second, smaller outbuilding about thirty feet away.

"What do you know about sewage?" Brossard was panting a little. I clawed some fir needles out of my hair. "Never thought about it, right? Flush and forget?" He poked me in the shoulder until I was facing the smaller shack. "Fine if you live in the city, but what about an island? What about here?" He nudged me in the calf. "Let's have a look."

Up close, the smaller building looked like a toolshed. Someone had taken a lot of trouble to make it look nice by nailing cedar shingles to the exterior walls. But the roof was just a sheet of cheap fiber-glass. Maybe they'd run out of shingles. Or money.

"It's not a toolshed," said Brossard, reading my mind again. "The guy who built it, his wife didn't want to see their sewage-treatment system every time she looked out the window. So he came up with this. Other people hide them under rocks. Or behind hedges. But it's still a tank of shit."

Brossard rifled through his ball of keys, unlocked the door and reached inside. A curly fluorescent bulb winked on and began to brighten. "Don't be shy," he said, grabbing my elbow and pulling me in. "I'm going to explain it, you're going to listen, and then you're going to get some time to think about Beethoven's Tenth Symphony."

"So you do know what you're looking for." There didn't seem any point in pretending.

"And I know you've got it. Now all we have to do is encourage you to make the right decision. So." He rubbed his small hands. "Pay attention, because this matters. See those manhole covers?"

You'd have had to be blind not to. Side by side, three feet across, they took up most of the floor. In one corner sat an untidy pile of cut two-by-fours, fuel for a woodstove perhaps. That was all there was.

"Two tanks. Two functions." Brossard pointed to the lid nearest him. "The main septic tank is under here. The other tank has the pump. Lost already? Let's have a look."

The covers were secured with small clamps. Brossard knelt, spun the clamps off and backhanded them out the door. He grabbed the edges of the main tank cover, thought better of it and stood again. "I'd hate for somebody to just kick me in," he said. "You open it."

Outwit, I thought. Outsmart. I got down where he'd been and grabbed the cool fiberglass edge of the lid.

"I hope you're up-to-date with your hepatitis shots." Brossard laughed.

The lid came off suddenly as the rubber seal released. I rocked back on my heels.

"Lean it up against the wall. We won't be needing it for a while. Now take a good look, because I'm only gonna tell you once."

The surface of the liquid inside the tank was a lumpy brown carpet that looked solid enough to walk on. It reminded me of the top of my grandmother's Christmas cake.

"They call that the crust," Brossard said, "but sometimes it's pretty soft. Technically, then, it's a scum. Got a cell phone?"

I fumbled in my jacket and handed it over. He wasn't going to search me. I still had Beethoven's manuscript. Outthink.

"Usually you test the crust with some kind of probe. But this'll do." He tossed my phone into the tank. It knifed through the surface layer and vanished.

"We'll call that one a scum," said Brossard. "Forget the phone—there's no reception here anyway."

I was already having difficulty concentrating, and it wasn't just the horror of the scum and what was trapped in it and how deep the tank extended beneath it. It was the smell. Like sour cabbage with a whiff of ammonia. It was invasive, instantly penetrating my clothes, my hair, my skin. If I ever got out of this shed, I would be showering for days. I struggled to listen to what Brossard was saying and tried not to breathe. He was gesturing at the tank.

"Everything dumps in there first. Toilet, sink, shower. The heavy stuff sinks. Bacteria gobble it up, and what's left is the liquid you're wrinkling your nose at. It's called effluent. Or gray water. The goop on the bottom is called sludge. Your phone sank through the gray water and ended up in the sludge. You think gray water stinks? Don't even think about the sludge." He peered at me. "You all right?"

I wasn't all right. I felt like throwing up. But I forced myself to play along. "Nothing's happening," I said. "In there."

"Good boy. The reason is there's no new crap going in. Bacteria got nothing to do. Don't worry. When I go into the house, you'll hear how it's supposed to sound."

"When you go into the house?"

"Too cold for me out here. Open the other tank. We're not finished yet."

I did as I was told. When I leaned the lid against the wall, something stabbed my hand. Whoever had shingled the shed had pounded the nails straight through the plywood wall. And they'd used nails that were too long for the job. Every couple of inches, a naked nail poked through. Floor to ceiling. It was like a medieval torture chamber.

I was inside an iron maiden with two tanks of shit.

Steps

The second tank smelled more or less like the first—as far as I could tell. By that time the whole shed was a stink bomb. It didn't seem to bother Brossard.

"This one is easy to understand," he said. "See that big pipe that runs from the main tank? It's a cascade system. The main tank fills up with effluent and overflows into this one, which gets emptied when the level triggers the pump. It all ends up in the Nanaimo sewer system. As long as your pump keeps working, you're fine."

"As long as your pump keeps working." The smell was making me light-headed.

"Ah! There it goes now." He held up a hand. A submarine-like whirring started up somewhere under my feet. The level of gray water in the pump tank began to fall. We watched it together.

"I really hate to do this," Brossard said. "Think of it as motivation." He seized a fistful of greasy wiring taped to the top of the pump and yanked. The bare ends sparked free. He tossed the ruined wiring into the gray water, stood up and rubbed his palms on his pants. I couldn't hear the pump anymore. But I still hadn't quite realized what that meant.

"I'm out of here," he said. "I need a drink. Start the woodstove, put my feet up." He grabbed the two tank lids and rolled them out the door. I heard them wobble and crash in the undergrowth. "Maybe a nice hot bath too," he said. Then he reached for the lightbulb and unscrewed it. Maybe he threw the bulb out the door, maybe he put it in his pocket—it didn't matter. I couldn't see my own hand in front of my face. I could hear his voice though. But now it came from outside the shed.

"Yell all you like. Cedar's a pretty good insulator. And there's nobody around anyway. I'll drop by in an hour or so." The door crunched shut, and I heard the lock click. Then a couple of footsteps, then nothing. I was alone in the dark with a crippled septic system.

I don't like the dark. I see things and I hear things, and I reach for a light switch before my imagination takes over completely. Don't move, I told myself now. Three minutes, your eyes will adapt, and you'll be able at least to see the edges of the tanks.

But most of the fiberglass roof was covered by clumps of moss and fir needles, and my wristwatch produced a pathetic two-inch circle of greenish illumination. So much for sight.

Of the remaining four senses, smell and taste were already overloaded. That left touch and hearing. And I was just about to conclude there was nothing to hear in there when I caught a faint rushing sound. It built to a sustained gurgle that was coming my way. Then something splashed into the main tank. My gorge rose and my heart sank. Brossard had flushed the toilet.

I had to hand it to him, he was a good teacher. When the trickle of gray water started to spill into the pump tank, I finally understood what was happening. And when the trickle faltered and something else began to come down the main pipe, I knew what Brossard was up to. He wasn't just going to flush the toilet. He was going to open every tap in the house, and he was going to take a nice hot bath and drain that at me too, and each gallon that left the house was going to drive the level in the pump tank higher, until it overflowed onto my shoes. Because there was no longer a pump to remove it.

Now the sound of water barreling into the main tank was a continuous muffled roar beneath the steady tinkling of the overflow. I jumped back, and a half dozen nail points stabbed me. Then I cautiously extended a foot in the dark until my shoe hit the rim of the tank. I had a few feet to work in. And no way of telling for how long.

I gently detached myself from the wall, did a careful pirouette and raised my hands so that I could lightly touch the protruding nails. Then I began to sidle crabwise, kicking out occasionally with a foot to pinpoint the tank locations. In five minutes I confirmed that every wall was perforated. Even the door was part of the iron maiden. The nails must go all the way to the roof, that dark smudge ten feet above me. My slow progress around the tanks was blocked only by the little pile of wood I'd seen when the light was still on. Even if I stood on the pile, there was no way I could reach the top. But that flimsy roof was my only hope.

The steady rushing of water into the main tank hadn't changed. But the trickling into the disabled pump tank was getting louder. I looked at my watch. Twenty minutes since Brossard had locked me in. The tank had to be close to overflowing. I backed up, holed myself on more nails and marveled at how acute my remaining senses had become. As the gray water crested the lip of the tank and began to course over the side, my ears told me exactly where it was heading. Toward me. I fumbled for the woodpile and grabbed one of the lengths of two-by-four. I wondered if maybe I could stack them—but that would only prolong the inevitable.

I flung the stick at the wall in frustration. There was no escape. Brossard had me.

He'd come back in an hour, and I'd stagger out and lay Beethoven's Tenth at those damned sandaled feet.

And then I realized there was something I *hadn't* heard. I'd thrown the stick, and it had hit the wall with a satisfying crunch. But I hadn't heard it fall. I fumbled for another one and let fly again. This one simply disappeared, only a soft thud marking the end of its flight. Outwit? Outsmart? I couldn't claim either of those. But I had definitely gotten lucky. Because what if it wasn't me that got driven onto those infernal nails? What if it was chunks of wood?

Plumbing 101

I put the first step at knee height, hammering one length of two-by-four with another until I knew it was impaled on at least four nails. Then a second, level with my belt, and a third at chin height. Enough for a test. I grasped the top step and gingerly transferred my weight to the bottom one. It held for an instant, then collapsed. My knee raked an exposed nail, and I was back where I'd started, bleeding. But when I felt for the step, it was still there. The problem was too much leverage; my weight was bending the nails. I heaved on the steps from underneath, forcing them upward and hammering them further onto the nails. I tried my weight again on the first step, and this time it held. The nails still started to bend, but slower than before. If I climbed fast, I might make it. Stopping to think would not be an option.

I hammered in six more steps, flailing desperately at the lethal carpet of nails in the darkness. I overbuilt, assuming half of the steps would fall off. The last two should take my head to the roof, I calculated, and to put them in I had to put all my weight on the bottom step. It groaned and gave out just as I finished pounding. I replaced it. Whenever I rested, all I could hear was the effluent coursing over the top of the tank and my own ragged breathing. My eyes streamed. Soon the air in here would be unbreathable.

You're a spider, I told myself. A spider in the woodshed in the dark. And spiders are too stupid to feel fear. When the effluent rose over the soles of my shoes, I knew it was now or never. I launched myself at the invisible wall and started to climb.

Halfway up, I heard Brossard coming down the path. I froze, splayed. *You're a very small spider.*

"Had enough?"

I could feel the step under my left foot beginning to sag. I eased my weight to the other foot, and that step started to fail too.

"Fuck you," I yelled. This was not the time for dialogue.

"Suit yourself." His voice was slurred.

I heard him crunch back up the path, and I started to count to ten. The step under my foot fell out at eight. I lunged for the next one. A nail punctured my shirt and raked through a few bars of Beethoven's Tenth, and I heard the splash of the fallen step. Then my head hit the roof, which lifted just enough for me to stab a hand through the crack.

I didn't care about steps now. Real spiders don't need steps. I got my other hand over the top, head-butted the flimsy fiberglass and sent a mental thank-you to the homeowner who'd lost interest in his job. The roof came loose easily, wet moss and needles sliding onto the ground and a wedge of blessed, sparkling December sky opening for me. I hauled my body up and over the wall and dropped to the ground.

Dirt had never smelled so good. I looked at my watch. I'd been inside the iron maiden for an hour.

But I'd escaped. And Beethoven was still with me. I knelt on the wet earth and let relief wash over me. And then I surprised myself. Because after that wave of emotion there came another, and it was even bigger. I'd always thought of myself as the guy who wouldn't—couldn't—hurt a fly. But I was a spider now. And I wanted to do some serious damage to someone.

Even from outside Brossard's cottage, I could hear water thundering down drains. I tiptoed over a rotten porch. The door was open, and I slid inside. A single room served for living, sleeping and cooking. A clothes-line ran from one corner to the other. I saw soiled long johns. The kitchen tap was wide open, and six empty beer bottles were lined up on the table next to his bunch of keys. But there was no Brossard. I crept toward the bathroom, shoes squelching.

I could have tap-danced into the room. Brossard was passed out in the bathtub, an empty bottle of Canadian Club whiskey between his legs and water drilling between his splayed feet. No wonder his voice had sounded slurred. His gun lay on the toilet seat, and I slid it into one of my pockets.

Anger welled up. Passed out like this, Brossard wouldn't have returned to that reeking shed before morning. What shape would I have been in after a freezing night out there? Brossard was going to pay. He'd given me all this practical knowledge of septic systems. Now he would eat his own words.

Brossard's kitchen drawers were even more chaotic than mine. I rummaged through them until I found a flashlight and some zip ties. I grabbed his keys. Back at the shed, I located the clamps, rolled both lids back inside and capped the tanks. The main tank was easy, but I had to kneel on the overflowing pump tank while I wrestled the clamps into place and tightened them. The vile torrent slowed to a trickle and stopped.

I ran back inside, grabbed one of Brossard's fat wrists and swiftly zip-tied it to the tap. One hand would be enough. One hand would make Brossard's next few hours even more interesting. A puffy eyelid opened a crack, then closed again.

I turned off the bathtub tap, grabbed a dirty towel from the clothesline and jammed it elbow-deep into Brossard's toilet bowl. Water was still going into the drains from the kitchen, but with the septic tanks sealed, the pump disabled and the toilet plugged, there was only one way the effluent could get out. One inlet, one outlet. I put my nose down between Brossard's feet and caught a familiar whiff from the drain. I'd just passed Plumbing 101. Retribution was on its way.

Drinking in the Bathtub

The last ferry from Protection Island left at ten. By the time I limped down the steep ramp to the dock, the boat was filling with liquored-up young men returning from a pre-Christmas visit to the pub. I stepped into a boozy haze, and the captain held out a hand for the fare. Then he jumped back.

"I can't take you," he said. "You'll have to leave the vessel."

The vessel was a converted lifeboat. Its captain was short and squinty, in shapeless, trod-on jeans. I was still buzzing with testosterone from my visit to Brossard's bathroom, and a petty tyrant was the last thing I needed. I yanked off my effluent-soaked shoes and threw them over the side. Then I tugged out my wallet and waved a pungent five-dollar bill at him.

"Dude, you took *us*," one of the drunk guys said. He weaved toward me until he got within range. "Whoa. Whaddya been drinking, fella?"

"Okay. Over there." The captain took the money and pointed to the end of the boat. A little river of passengers parted, and I sat down heavily next to the engine exhaust. The drunks at the front gave me a ragged cheer. A few flakes of snow swirled in the door.

By the time I'd walked back to my apartment, my socks had frozen. I couldn't feel my toes. I stood in a warm shower while sensation pinpricked back into my feet. Then I ran a stick of deodorant over as much of my body as I could reach, got dressed, stuffed my stinking clothes in a garbage bag and went out. I slung the bag in the Dumpster and headed for The Loft. Beethoven stayed behind in his moist envelope under the bed. He didn't smell so good.

I knew the way to The Loft, but I still had the sensation that I was entering new territory. Familiar streets look different when you think someone's after you. Not knowing who it is makes you walk faster. Worst of all, not being responsible for any of it makes you feel like the street is being pulled out from under your feet. It was a good time for a chat with a sympathetic bartender.

Kaz was behind the bar, fussing with his bottles of wood polish and chatting with the cop Tina and a man sitting next to her. The new guy kept nodding and laughing as though he wanted to belong but couldn't figure out how. Another cop? I had a fleeting vision of Brossard in his bathtub and pushed it out of my head. The bastard had locked me in a freezing shed with an overflowing septic tank. He deserved what I'd done to him, even if it was slightly illegal.

I sat next to Tina. She seemed happy to see me, then puzzled, and then she wound her scarf around the lower half of her face. At least her eyes were smiling. Kaz set a whiskey in front of me.

"Septic failure," he said. Kaz can be insufferable.

"Is there anything you don't know?" I took a sip, and my insides lit up like a blast furnace. I realized I was still cold.

"Which is interesting, because Nanaimo doesn't have a septic system," Kaz went on. Now Tina and her friend were watching. Effluent must have been coming out of my pores. I drank some more whiskey.

"I worked at the pub on Protection Island when I first came here," Kaz said. "Protection Island has a septic system. Quite a unique one."

I tried to imagine Kaz mixing margaritas to country and western music. Tina unwound the scarf. Behind it was an amused smile. It was a pretty nice smile. "Welcome back," she said. "This is Barry. Also with the force. I'm trying to raise the culture bar down at headquarters." The guy grinned sheepishly. He looked like he'd be more at home in the Protection Island pub.

"So, Frank," said Tina. "Maybe there's something you'd like to share with us? Off the record?"

I saw Brossard again in his bathtub. "Just a conversation-in-a-bar sort of thing?"

"Just like that."

I downed my drink and then told them everything. When I'd finished, I pulled Brossard's gun out of my jacket and slid it onto the bar. Tina stirred it in a circle with a slender finger. She wore her nails short, so I guessed the cherry nail polish was compensation.

"Oh boy," she said. Kaz picked up the gun and broke it open. All of a sudden it looked a little small, even in Kaz's hands.

"This is a tagging gun," Tina said. The amused smile was back. "Fisheries uses them to mark salmon. The worst he could have done was put a spaghetti tag in your ass."

I began to feel foolish. "What was an ex-cop doing with a fish gun?"

"Did he say he was an ex-cop?"

"Not in so many words."

Tina looked at her colleague. He shrugged. Then she turned back to me. "Bob Brossard used to be a Fisheries enforcement officer. Government laid him off, along with a bunch of other Fisheries people. He went a bit nuts for a while. Then he started this stupid business as a private dick."

"So you know him."

"This is Nanaimo. Of course we know him." She looked at her watch, drained her beer and thumped her colleague on the shoulder. "Duty calls," she said. "I knew coming here was too good to be true."

She turned back to me. "Don't go away. We'll be back in time for your last set." And she gave me the smile again. This time it wasn't a half smile. It was a real one.

"Sounds like your private detective's out of commission for the next few days," Kaz said when they'd left. "The Beethoven conference starts tomorrow. We should be fine."

"We?"

Kaz produced his own half smile. "You've forgotten? I promised I'd make some inquiries in Tokyo. About collectors, people who might be interested in Beethoven's Tenth."

"I thought we agreed just about everybody would be interested."

"Yeah, but interested enough to hire people to rough somebody up? That narrows it down." Kaz looked smug.

"Sounds like you've narrowed it."

"Go play your set," Kaz said. "Just don't fraternize too much with my customers." He touched the side of his nose.

Tina came back in just as I was finishing. She was alone. The Loft was nearly full, and when I got over to the bar it was so crowded that I had to squeeze in beside her. She looked at me and rolled her eyes. In a nice sort of way.

"You had me fooled," she said. "I never figured you for the new Bruce Willis."

"You found him." I already felt relieved.

"Barry found him. I was out looking at your little climbing wall. Nice. I just love a man who can use tools." She winked. "Then Barry starts yelling from the house. Actually, he wasn't amused. I had to talk him out of laying charges."

"Why? The bastard kidnapped me."

"Charges against *you*."

"Me?"

"Brossard wasn't doing so well. The bathtub was full of freezing sewage. He was hanging half out of it. He'd tried to cut through the zip tie with a broken bottle, but he made better progress on his hand. He was passed out. Hypothermia and loss of blood."

"You're not supposed to drink in the bathtub." I couldn't believe I'd said that. But it felt pretty good.

Tina put two fingers on my arm. "I like your playing. Really. But do me a favor? Keep your head down for a week or so. We had to call in the paramedics, the harbor patrol made a trip over, it's damn near Christmas, and so far I've convinced Barry to call it a suicide attempt." She did that slow smile again. "Compounded by a drain malfunction."

"So I'm guessing your colleague won't be back to hear me play?"

"You'd better hope not," said Tina. "Stick to music. Please."

"Okay. I'll stick to music."

Kaz came by, removed Tina's empty and wordlessly placed two fresh beers in front of us. When he straightened, I caught his eye. We'd soon be in Vancouver. I was starting to like Tina. But I knew it was going to be hard to keep my promise to her.

Senior Citizen

After I'd finished my last set, I helped Kaz collect empties and stack them in the dishwasher. Tina had left, probably to go home and take a long shower. Kaz gave his beloved bar a final wipe and set a laptop on the gleaming surface.

"They caught Stefan," he said. "It'll be in the news tomorrow. Thought you'd like to know."

"I'd like to know how you know."

"Sources." Kaz gave me his enigmatic smile. "The guy was wandering around in the grocery store with a concussion. Apparently, his fingerprints were all over the apartment where that old lady was killed. So as far as bad guys are concerned, we're two down."

There was that *we* again.

"And one to go." He did some typing and a fuzzy headshot appeared on the screen. "Remember when I said I'd talk to my contacts in Japan? It took me a couple of hours, but I found the right guy. You owe me for some long distance calls."

"And?"

"My contact's name is Fujimori-san. Made his millions in tuna futures. Now he's one of the top collectors of rare manuscripts. Deep pockets, low profile."

"Is that why his picture's so fuzzy? He doesn't even look Asian."

"This isn't Fujimori-san. There are no pictures of Fujimori-san on the Internet. This is someone else."

"Don't tell me. There aren't any pictures of this guy either."

"Nope. Fujimori-san sent this one to me. He thinks this is the person who has the last movement of Beethoven's Tenth."

I pulled the laptop closer. "Your friend is right," I said. I dug in my breast pocket. "But I've got a better picture. Two, in fact." I handed him the Pieczynski family portraits. Kaz held them next to the miserable photo on the screen. He traced the faint outline of the birthmark.

"His name is Klaus Pfiffner," he said. "Rumored to have escaped to South America just before the end of the war." He tapped the image of the unsmiling Miss P. in frock and ringlets. "That must be the sister."

"Now deceased."

"The rumor is that Pfiffner's father was very high up in the party. He had access to all the artworks the Nazis looted during the war. The story goes he split Beethoven's Tenth into two parts. Klaus got the last movement. Your late friend got the rest.

Dad shot himself when the Allies entered Berlin."

"And his son sneaked out of the country. Sixty years later he puts a hit on his own sister." The image onscreen was so bad it could have been of anyone. "No wonder she hid the picture. She must have changed her name too. He doesn't look evil though, does he?"

"He's probably in his mid-eighties now, Fujimori-san thinks. He'd have a tough time traveling all the way from South America. Fujimori-san would love to talk to him though. And to us, of course."

"That's up to Fujimori," I said. "All I care about is that we don't seem to have a problem anymore." Now I was the one saying *we*. I took back the family photos. "I need some sleep. Tomorrow I'm going to Vancouver. There's a pre-conference lecture in the evening, open to the public. Perfect for us. You're still coming?"

Kaz closed the laptop on Miss P.'s unpleasant brother. "I wouldn't miss it," he said. "I'm going over first thing to buy some supplies for the restaurant. I'll pick you up at the ferry terminal. Don't forget the manuscript."

"Very funny," I said.

* * *

It was late when I got back to my apartment. Klaus Pfiffner was able to travel after all. He was standing in front of my door.

"Frank's not home," I said. "And his door has a deadbolt."

Pfiffner withdrew the plastic shim he was wiggling in the seam and turned to face me. He was stooped and frail-looking, his body lost in a cheap winter coat two sizes too big. The kind of coat a visitor from South America would use once and throw away. A yellow scarf was wound around his neck so that his small, shaven head protruded like a bean. The birth-mark was coarse and pitted now, and he'd tried to cover it in flesh-colored makeup. But Pfiffner's flesh was the wrong color to begin with. It was gray.

The hall door banged open, and Mrs. Horowitz, my TV-watching neighbor, scurried past us and started wrestling with her own door. For once I was happy to see her.

"Then you must give Mr. Ryan a message." Pfiffner's voice startled me. It was deep and still powerful, a parade-ground voice. His English was accented with a weird mixture of German and Spanish, and his breath was metallic. "Tell him that what he has belongs to my family. Tell him also that that I know what he plans to do with it. Tell him, finally, that I have money. That I can save him a lot of trouble."

Mrs. Horowitz kept fiddling with her lock. She was taking it all in. Pfiffner tugged the oversized coat around himself and began to walk away. Then, without turning around, he said, "Maybe I even save his life."

"You killed your own sister."

Pfiffner stopped, and this time he turned around. "My sister was uncooperative. As your friend appears to be." Then he slowly opened the heavy fire door and disappeared. Mrs. Horowitz suddenly found the right key and vanished.

I double-bolted the door behind me and poured a whiskey I knew I would regret. Then I took the glass to the window and watched Klaus Pfiffner emerge from the building, foreshortened and dwarf-like, the yellow streetlight reflecting off his head. It took him a long time to shuffle to the end of the block, turn and disappear.

Beethoven's Tenth was where I'd left it, under the bed. I moved the envelope to the piano so the smell wouldn't interfere with my sleep. Because I was able to sleep now. Stefan and Brossard were off the street. Their boss had made it all the way from South America, I'd give him that. But after my adventure on Protection Island, I figured I could handle a geriatric ex-Nazi in a thrift-shop overcoat. Even Mrs. Horowitz had been enough to scare him off. Beethoven's birthday was almost here, and I was going to enjoy every minute of it.

Easy Come

In the morning I bought a new cell phone, called Kaz and told him I'd be on the late-afternoon ferry to Horseshoe Bay. He was already scurrying around Vancouver, buying bulk noodles or beer coasters or whatever it was that kept him in business. I headed for the ferry terminal wearing my best shoes, a winter jacket and an overnight bag slung over my shoulder.

Our plan was to drive into Vancouver, grab a quick bite at one of the obscure restaurants Kaz seemed to know and head over to the public Beethoven session, which was being held downtown at the

Vancouver Art Gallery. Assorted experts were scheduled to speak, followed by a question-and-answer. That was when I planned to stand up and have my *ta-da!* moment. And after a sleepless night with Miss P.'s ghost, I still wasn't sure if that moment would, or should, result in money in my pocket.

The walk to the ferry terminal took half an hour. I could tell it was going to be one of those rough winter crossings. Already the wind was funneling down Newcastle Channel, and the big swells would be building out in the unprotected Strait of Georgia. In the distance, Protection Island was just an unthreatening green smudge. Woodstoves sent up wavering columns of smoke.

I looked back once or twice. But there were no evil pensioners doddering along behind me. If Pfiffner was determined enough to shadow me, he'd be boarding the ferry on foot. The big waiting lounge made it easy for me to monitor the passengers, and I walked onto the ship last, just to be sure. No Nazis.

I got a good seat in the restaurant, bought a coffee and settled in as the big ship detached from the dock and headed for the rough waters of the strait. All around me families filled the other tables. Pre-Christmas traveling, I figured. I wondered how many of them would care about the present strapped to my stomach. You never knew. Maybe for one of these people, Beethoven's Tenth would be life-changing.

I turned to an elderly woman sitting at the next table.

"Can you watch my bag?" I needed another coffee. Three hours' sleep is too little, even for me. She smiled, nodded and went back to her knitting. By the time I got back, the ferry was juddering through waves that even from the comfortable restaurant looked remorseless. For the rest of the crossing, people would stay put.

The ferry slammed and shook. Cutlery slid across tables. By the time we finally approached the lee of the mainland, my bladder was bursting. I shouldered my bag and lurched off in search of a washroom. Someone was groaning inside one of the stalls. I smelled vomit. I wedged myself between two urinals and fumbled with my clothing.

That was when Pfiffner got me. I felt an unholy, searing pain in one buttock and smelled his acrid breath. Then a slight tug at my shoulder and he was gone. I clutched my ass with one hand and struggled to finish relieving myself with my right. Behind me a cubicle door opened, and somebody staggered out.

My bottom was on fire. I danced in front of the mirror, trying to see it. Where had Pfiffner come from? I rapidly revised my opinion of him. Whatever he had stabbed me with, he knew how to use it. I had to be bleeding like a tormented bull.

I hammered at the towel dispenser and it spat out a long brown ribbon. I crumpled the paper, stuffed it inside my boxers and pounded out two more lengths for later.

Now they were announcing our arrival in Horseshoe Bay. I limped into the happy crowd, wounded but presentable. Pfiffner hadn't gotten my cell phone. I texted Kaz.

"He's on the ferry. He got my bag. And me. Am walking slowly." I started the shuffle toward the exit. I didn't see Pfiffner in the crowd, and I didn't expect to. He might be a geezer, but he was obviously a professional. Maybe he'd hide somewhere on the ship. Maybe he'd just pay again and ride back in comfort, which was probably what he'd been doing all day. Sailing back and forth, waiting for his target to walk into the trap. I didn't care how he'd done it.

All I cared about was making it to Kaz's car. The pain was so intense I was having trouble thinking.

Kaz's dented Subaru was idling in a No Parking zone. "He didn't get off," Kaz said. His face was set in a way I'd not seen before. I got into the front seat, twisting and turning in an effort to find a comfortable position. When I looked up I saw Pfiffner high above us, scuttling along the gantry that ran alongside the ferry.

"Take a right. He's heading for the village," I said. City buses stopped in Horseshoe Bay—that's how he would get away. One transfer to the airport and he'd be gone. "Go!"

Kaz accelerated hard between two semi-trailers grinding down the off-ramp, skidded onto the first exit and barreled into the village. I wondered if I should add race-car driver to his list of skills. I picked out Pfiffner again, walking fast along the seawall that led to town. The oversized coat flapped in the stiff wind. When he saw us bearing down on him, he jumped nimbly onto the long board-walk that led, high above the water, to the Horseshoe Bay Marina. Pfiffner was full of surprises.

But he had no way out. Kaz snapped through the wooden barrier and bore down on the small figure, tires moaning on the wooden planks. Pfiffner reached the end and wheeled around. He was cornered, and he knew it. I grabbed my bleeding buttock and struggled out of the car as Kaz went for him.

Then Pfiffner brought an envelope out of my shoulder bag. He held it aloft, like a soccer referee showing a red card. Kaz stopped in his tracks. Pfiffner upended the envelope and Beethoven's Tenth shot free, the wind catching the wheeling pages. Most of them settled in the black water below. I watched a few, caught in a sudden updraft, circle and land on the beach. But all of it was lost.

Kaz was on Pfiffner instantly. I grabbed Kaz's arm. Pfiffner wasn't putting up any resistance—suddenly he was an old man again. Kaz would kill him.

"What's the point?" I said. "It's over."

We watched Miss P.'s brother shuffle back down the boardwalk and disappear into the village. I pulled a bloodied wad of paper towel out of my pants and replaced it with a new one. Then we got back into Kaz's car. The rear seat was piled with noodles.

Neither of us spoke until we had crossed the Lions Gate Bridge and were entering the neon of downtown Vancouver. It began to snow. Kaz looked serene again. And he was driving at the speed limit.

"Cheer up," I said. "He obviously didn't have time to look too closely at it. And old people have terrible eyesight."

Easy Go

We turned up busy Denman Street into the West End. "The pressure's off now," I said. "Let's get some dinner. Somewhere interesting. And with a decent bathroom."

We pulled over at London Drugs, and I ran in to buy a box of Depends. The girl at the till gave me a searching look.

"They're not for me," I said.

"You're awfully quiet," I told Kaz when I crawled back into the car. "It's my problem, you know. Not yours."

Kaz was peering out the window, slowing and then speeding up as he searched for just the right restaurant. They all looked the same to me in this part of town. Neon sign, a lantern or two, menus posted at the door, young Asian people coming and going. I didn't care. When it came to restaurants, Kaz was the authority.

"What did you mean?" he said, still peering. "About him not having much time?"

"He got to me just as the ferry was about to dock. By the time I was out of the washroom, people were lining up to leave. He had time to make sure the manuscript was in my bag. But not enough time to look closely at it."

If Kaz was listening, he didn't show it. Suddenly he veered into one of those empty parking spaces that never appear for me in Vancouver. "Here," he said.

The place was nondescript. But when I pulled the door open we were met with a blast of sound and grill smoke. The servers yelled at us. Kaz nodded and smiled. "It's a greeting," he said. "Standard practice for an izakaya."

"A what?" Now the servers were yelling at the chefs, who were hopping around behind a huge wooden bar. I hoped Kaz wouldn't pull out a rag and start polishing it. I couldn't hear myself think.

"Izakaya. Japanese comfort food. Beer. Sake." Two places miraculously appeared at the crowded bar. Kaz took a long pull at one of the beers that materialized in front of us along with steaming hand towels. I did the same and then went to the bathroom to put a diaper on.

When I got back, Kaz was accepting two steaming plates from one of the chefs. Whatever it was, it smelled good. "You were saying?" he said.

I sat down carefully. At least the bleeding had slowed. "If he'd taken a closer look he would have realized it was a copy. The one in my bag. Not a bad copy. I mean, I went to some trouble to get the paper right. But yeah. A copy." The beer went down easily. I chopsticked one of the morsels into my mouth. It was a small silver fish, slashed, salted and grilled.

"You eat the head too," said Kaz.

I ate the head.

"Where's the original?" he said.

I fumbled in my shirt and pulled out the envelope. It was damp again from all my exertions. And it still smelled a little. I laid it on the bar next to me. Kaz glanced at it and went on eating.

"Then we're back in business," he said with his mouth full.

"Yup." I was pretty pleased with myself. "If Pfiffner was on that ferry, I figured he'd go for whatever I was carrying. And he did." I looked at my watch. "We've only got forty-five minutes."

"No problem," he said. "Izakayas are basically fast-food restaurants. Except that the food is actually good."

I had to agree. We stuffed ourselves with eel and eggplant tempura and shimmering cubes of steamed tofu with curly pink shavings of dried bonito writhing on top. We even polished off a flagon of hot sake before Kaz went into his nodding rigamarole with the chefs, and suddenly we were heading for the door. Everybody yelled at us again. Then we were outside in the street. I was weaving slightly. But I felt good. The food had been good. Sitting there with a friend had been good, especially after everything I'd been through. And I had Beethoven's Tenth under my arm. There wasn't any reason to hide it now.

"I think I'll walk," said Kaz. He didn't seem to be weaving. "It's only a couple of blocks."

That seemed like a good idea to me. I said so.

"And I'll just take that." He plucked the envelope from under my arm and set off down Robson in the direction of the art gallery.

"It's okay," I said, trying to catch up. I really did feel light-headed. "I've carried it this far."

Kaz stopped and turned. He didn't look drunk at all. And he didn't look like Kaz anymore. At least, not the Kaz I knew.

"No. I mean, I'll take it. I am taking it." Something flickered across his face, a tiny grimace. "Sorry," he said. Then the old Kaz was gone for good. I limped in my diaper after the new one. He turned south on Howe and joined the crowd of people converging on the gallery entrance. A huge illuminated portrait of Beethoven looked down on them. He was frowning, and I thought, I'm with you, Ludwig. I caught up with Kaz just as he went through the door. The envelope had vanished somewhere. Maybe it was inside his own unwrinkled shirt. I grabbed his elbow, but I knew I could never win a struggle with him.

"Give my regards to Fujimori," I finally said.

"It's Fujimori-san to you."

"And get yourself another pianist."

"I won't need any more pianists," he said. "What did you think I was anyway? Your faithful servant? Your inscrutable Asian sidekick?" He shook his arm free.

"How about friend?" I said.

Kaz laughed. It wasn't a pleasant sound. "Do you have any clue what this thing is worth at auction? The original? In Beethoven's hand?"

I'd thought about the money. A lot. But in the end, I'd been too busy dodging thugs and climbing around septic tanks to come up with much of a plan. Anyway, the manuscript wasn't mine—it was Miss P.'s. If I'd had any plan at all, it was just to let the world know the symphony existed. And take it from there.

I started to tell Kaz, but he was gone, absorbed into the mass of people. I beat my way back out like a salmon swimming upstream. Then I stood outside until the stream dried up and someone finally shut the doors. It was snowing hard now. Kaz was inside with Beethoven's Tenth. I was alone in Vancouver with a box of Depends.

Iron Gall

I splurged and spent the night at the Hotel Vancouver across the street. I was feeling sorry for myself, and it was the kind of place where they didn't ask questions if you showed up with nothing but a box of diapers. I slept on three layers of the finest hotel towels. At least I'd stopped leaking. When I woke up it was after nine, and snow was still falling on West Georgia Street. Downtown Vancouver looked magical.

The hotel provided early editions of both city newspapers, and I bundled them under my arm and set off in search of a warm café. There was one right around the corner, as there generally is in Vancouver. I toasted my return to normal life with strong coffee, a croissant and the news.

Beethoven's birthday was on the front page of the Arts section in both newspapers, but there was nothing about his Tenth Symphony. And that was odd. Why would Fujimori not take advantage of such a golden opportunity for making his latest acquisition known to the world? The publicity alone would have been priceless.

Maybe there was something about the manuscript that I'd missed. Was it a fake? I doubted that. It was old, it seemed to be in Beethoven's hand, and it had been examined by a musician who knew his Beethoven, even if he didn't play him much. And there couldn't be anything physically wrong, because that manuscript had hardly been out of my sight since Miss P. handed it to me. I'd been through hell and high water with the thing. In and out of bars and cars and boats and overflowing septic tanks. Apart from a couple of nights spent under my bed, that manuscript had literally never left my side. I still found myself reaching down to check on it.

I decided to stop thinking about it. The table was a mess of newspapers, and my fingers were black with ink. Why couldn't printers use something that lasted a bit longer? I got up to wash them and suddenly thought, Ink. Newspaper ink dissolves on your fingers. The ink in a book doesn't. What about the ink on a two-hundred-year-old manuscript?

In thirty seconds I was across the road and running my finger down the list of offices in the Vancouver Art Gallery. Galleries had conservators, people whose job it was to protect old things. Pictures, frames, documents. And there he was, K. Aronson, office on the mezzanine level. I took the steps two at a time.

It was ten o'clock in the morning. K. Aronson was a civil servant. His door opened right on time. Aronson was in his fifties, with a dirty gray ponytail and a stoop. He wore a cardigan, faded jeans and purple ladies' pumps.

"Buy you a coffee?" I said.

Aronson blinked and shrugged. He was obviously used to dealing with the public. "Why not? Just promise not to show me your mother's lost Emily Carr."

Five minutes later I was back at the same table in the café across the street. I felt better now that Aronson's feet were also under it.

"What do you know about old ink?" I asked. "And old paper?"

"Old meaning what?" He took a bite of the pastry I'd bought him, and flakes showered onto the table between us. "A hundred years? Three hundred?"

"Two hundred," I said.

"Don't tell me. You've got the original Articles of Confederation under your shirt."

"Early nineteenth century," I said, leaning forward. "Music manuscript, probably written in Germany."

Aronson gave me an appraising look and bit into his pastry again. I jumped back.

"That period, that place, most likely it's iron gall ink. Beautiful ink. Writing sort of brownish?"

I nodded.

"Faded? A little halo around each letter?"

I nodded.

"Iron gall then. The paper would be brittle by now."

"It was. I mean, it is."

Another look. "That's all you want to know?" He glanced at his watch.

"One more thing. How do you preserve something like that?"

"Control the temperature. Watch the humidity. Lots of air circulation. No heat, no moisture, no acids. Preservation is easy. Restoration is hard. Once it starts to go, the ink just basically rusts through the paper, and it all falls apart."

"But it's a slow process, right?"

Aronson laughed. "Depends how hard you try. Sit in the sauna with something like that and you could fry it in two days." He stood up and brushed pastry flakes onto my lap. "Look, good luck with it. And thanks for the coffee."

"Good luck with what?"

"You're the second person today asking me about iron gall ink. Make that the third. Two guys were waiting for me outside my door when I got to work this morning. I had a look at their manuscript. It smelled worse than some saunas I've been in. And it was unreadable."

He began to thread his way through the crowd of coffee-breaking office workers. I had a sudden image of Aronson in a sauna. In ladies' shoes. He turned. "No honor among thieves, eh?"

Heat, humidity, acidic conditions. That pretty much described the world under my shirt for the last four days. Right about now, Fujimori and Kaz were probably huddled somewhere in Vancouver, and it wouldn't be as nice as where I was now. Fujimori would be wanting his money back. I wondered how much he'd paid.

Maybe Miss P. had made a copy. Maybe it was still somewhere in her apartment, and Stefan had missed it. I'd made two copies myself—I'd have been out of my mind not to—and the other one was in a safety deposit box in Nanaimo. But I had a strong feeling it was never going to leave. Maybe, if I grew up and had kids, I'd will it to them and let them sort it out. As it stood now, I had the copy but not the original, and Kaz had the original but no copy.

Pfiffner still had the final movement, the Presto, but that was a long way from an entire symphony. Beethoven's Last Movement?

Sounded more like a footnote. Beethoven's Tenth wasn't technically gone, but it looked like it would remain a curiosity. Pfiffner wasn't going to get rich off it. Neither was I. That was probably why Miss P. had chosen me in the first place—she knew I'd flub the money part. Anyway, I'd ruined the original, so I probably didn't deserve any reward. Nobody would get rich. I decided I liked that.

I folded up the newspapers. All around me, well-dressed people had the crazed look of big-city dwellers with only a few days to go before Christmas. Deals to be made, projects to finish, presents to buy. I wasn't sure I belonged in Nanaimo anymore, but I knew I didn't belong here. Maybe it was time to start a new life. Kaz would have to. He'd probably just take his abundant skills somewhere else, maybe open a bar or restaurant somewhere farther north.

For me, moving a couple of hundred miles might not be enough. There were lots of places in the world with pianos that needed tuning. And plenty of jazz lovers. Maybe a cruise ship, somewhere where I didn't have to ruin my shoes in rain and slush, where at the end of my gig I could stand at the rail and stare at the Southern Cross and think cosmic thoughts. Cruise ships had multiple bars and lounges, and I could throw in the tuning as a bonus.

I stood up, and my punctured buttock let out a silent whimper. True, most cruise-ship passengers were senior citizens, and I'd miss having a fan like Officer Tina. Come to think of it, I'd miss Tina, period. But at least senior citizens weren't dangerous.

Most of them.

Acknowledgments

My thanks to Terry Gordon for his explanation of the eccentricities of the Protection Island sewage system. Thanks also to everyone at Orca Book Publishers who helped bring this book to life, in particular, Ruth Linka, whose dead-on editing has made *Beethoven's Tenth* leaner, a bit meaner and just plain better. As always, David Greer read the early drafts, fed me ideas and kept me on course.

BRIAN HARVEY is a scientist and writer. He holds a PhD in marine biology and specializes in conservation of aquatic biodiversity. He founded and ran a successful nonprofit fisheries organization between 1995 and 2005, then resigned in order to devote more time to writing. Brian began his writing career in the mid-1990s with *Against the Current*, a travel column for the Victoria *Times Colonist* newspaper. He followed that with another column, *Reality Check*, for *Waters* magazine, as well as science-travel articles for *Escape* and *Westworld*. His first nonfiction book for a general audience, *The End of the River*, was chosen as a Globe and Mail Best 100 Book for 2008. He is currently finishing a second nonfiction book about sailing around Vancouver Island and is working on several fiction projects. Brian lives in Nanaimo, British Columbia.

TOKYO GIRL

A Frank Ryan Mystery

BY BRIAN HARVEY

Coming Fall 2016

An excerpt from Toyko Girl

"That's *so* much better," I said, trying to make it sound like I meant it. At the keyboard, Mrs. Ogawa made a quick ducking motion, as though someone had zinged a baseball at her head. I'm pretty sure this meant *I know you're lying. But thanks anyway.* She folded her small hands in her lap and awaited instructions.

Mrs. Ogawa's husband was a wholesaler of fish cakes in the famous Tsukiji seafood market. Or something like that. I'd never met him. Even if I had, I probably wouldn't have asked about his place of business. If I'd known that my last night in Japan would be spent in his fish market, I would have.

His wife had her heart set on learning "Clair de Lune," by Claude Debussy. We'd been at it together for two months and were closing in on page three. I didn't have the heart to tell her what was coming on page four. Mrs. Ogawa had applied herself equally hard to learning English, so we could communicate after a fashion, but these piano lessons were a challenge for both of us.

Mrs. Ogawa paid me well. So did the other Mrs. Ogawas who'd seen my ad and convinced their husbands to allow a *gaijin*— a foreigner—into the family home for a weekly shot of culture. I wanted to give her her money's worth. But it was in moments like this that I felt the most alien in Japan. Real communication seemed remote.

"We need a little more emotion," I finally said. "You know what I mean? Emotion?"

Mrs. Ogawa looked at her hands, and her head bobbed ever so slightly. Everyone knew what emotions were, even if they dealt with them differently. "May I?" I tapped her on the shoulder, and she shot to attention. I slid onto the piano bench.

"Lake. Moon. You're all alone." She stood behind me, and I played the first few bars. "Clair de Lune" really is a beautiful piece, no matter how many corny arrangements you've heard. I could hear Mrs. Ogawa breathing behind me. Or maybe it was the Chuo Expressway. I decided to let Debussy do the talking. I didn't stop until I'd played the whole piece through.

Then I just sat there. Mrs. Ogawa's breathing sounded different. I turned around. She had one hand over her nose and mouth. There were tear tracks on both cheeks. She sniffed. The lesson was over.

"Thank you, Frank-*san*," she said from behind her hand. She darted into her miniature kitchen, extracted five thousand yen from a drawer the way she always did and presented the banknotes to me formally, with both hands and a little bow. Japan was still a cash-dominated society. Every housewife seemed to have her own private stash somewhere. One of my students kept it underneath the rice cooker.

Being a tourist in Japan was easy. In my case, I'd needed to disappear somewhere safe. Japan was a no-brainer.

After what had happened to me in Nanaimo, I'd started seeing villains everywhere. My gig as a late-night jazz pianist was over. I started giving the harbor a wide berth in case someone might snatch me there again. Just opening my apartment door involved double-checking the latch, a lot of deep breaths and one hand on the bear spray I kept in my pocket. It was too bad. I'd liked Nanaimo. The city fit me like an old pair of jeans. But I'd tripped over those frayed cuffs, and I needed out.

According to the Internet, my chances of being assaulted or kidnapped were lowest in the Nordic countries, in New Zealand and in Japan. It was snowing in Nanaimo when I did my research, and Denmark or Sweden would just be more of the same. No thanks. All the pictures of New Zealand looked just like British Columbia, and I wanted change. That left Japan, where even if you got incredibly unlucky and someone bopped you over the head, he'd probably say "Excuse me" first.

But what if I ran into Kaz Nakamura? Statistics took care of that one. Japan had almost 127 million people. The mathematical odds of meeting Kaz were a bullet train of zeroes with a lonely numeral one at the end. Kaz and I had parted ways on a snowy night in Vancouver, and I would never see him again.

I gave my Nanaimo landlord three months' rent and bought a ticket for Tokyo. I arrived at the end of March, just two weeks after an earthquake under the Pacific Ocean had driven a fifty-foot wall of water—a tsunami—through the coastal city of Fukushima. The tidal wave hurdled a seawall, tossed freighters and ferries ashore like bathtub toys, left buses on hospital roofs and turned a nuclear power plant into a leaking radioactive time bomb. Japan had obviously used up its statistical share of bad luck. I would be fine.

And I was. You couldn't blame the country for being twitchy about aftershocks and radiation, and maybe that's why nobody paid much attention to me. Every week I moved to a cheaper hotel, drifting through the enormous city like a candy wrapper on a windy day.

That was two months ago. Now I was sitting in a noodle shop three minutes from Akiko's house, fueling up. You can't go wrong with a bowl of ramen. This place was typical: a scarred wooden counter with six stools and a grim-looking guy in a headband behind it, in a cloud of steam, flinging noodles and vegetables and slices of pork into bowls of his secret broth.

I ordered a Kirin. The place was full of men hoovering wet noodles. I never could do the slurping thing—usually, I ended up speckling my shirt with broth. They kept their eyes on the TV high up in one corner. On the screen, a man in a suit was saying something alarming about radiation. I knew it was alarming because Japanese TV news features graphics, exclamation marks and endlessly repeated footage of scenes of disaster. I finished my beer, left a thousand-yen note on the counter and headed around the corner into the stylish residential area where Akiko lived.

In the Ota district, the streets were narrow and painted with bewildering markings: arrows, dashes, dots, diamonds, numbers. From the street, Akiko's house was a slanted field of shiny blue roof tiles above an iron gate set into a stone wall. The silver Lexus in the tiled carport looked as though it had never left the showroom. I pushed the unmarked button set into the wall, waited for the gate to swing silently open, then walked along a path of crushed stone through a manicured glade with dwarf cypresses that trailed over a mossy pool.

I squatted and watched two koi chase each other's tails beneath a sprinkling of cherry petals. One fish was white with dramatic splashes of red, like blood. The other was a solid-gold submarine.

"Do you like fish, Frank?"

Akiko's bare brown toes were right next to me. I struggled to my feet. She knelt and paddled a long finger in the water, and the golden fish turned majestically to nuzzle it. "This one is my favorite. I call him Sunshine."

"I wouldn't know what to do with a pet fish," I said.

Akiko stood and smiled. That smile was the only part of her I felt comfortable with. It was lopsided. Maybe the surgeon had slipped. Somebody else had slipped too, and recently, because one of Akiko's remanufactured eyes was the color of a ripe fig. It was also swollen shut. She caught me looking, but her smile never wavered.

"I walked into a door," she said. I followed her ponytail across the polished flagstones. Each step left a fleeting footprint on the hot stone, as though she'd been waiting for me in the refrigerator.

Akiko's piano was better than anything I could ever have owned, a full nine gleaming feet that sat on a purple Persian rug. I sank into a cool leather chair and watched her bare feet go up and down on the Yamaha's pedals. Someone needed to tell Akiko to wear shoes to play piano, but it wasn't going to be me. She was playing Chopin, one of his weepier Preludes, a piece we'd been working on for a month. I wondered what it was like to read music with one eye.

The notes were all there, but I knew without even looking at Akiko that something was missing. Akiko had talent, but today she had tension too. Not a good combination for a musician.

I got up. I took one slender, locked wrist in my fingers. "Don't stop playing," I said. "Try to let go."

But she did stop. And it wasn't because I was bent over her wrist like a kindly doctor. It was because there was someone else in the room.